THE QUARTERDECK LADDER

Jeremiah Coghlan's meteoric rise from ship's boy to Post Captain in the Royal Navy of Nelson's time is a matter of historical fact. So is the succession of sea-fights by which he achieved his ambition. But navy records naturally have nothing to say about the private life of this obscure and forgotten hero, and here the author has interwoven fiction with fact to produce a stirring tale in which troubled romance ashore contrasts with desperate action afloat.

THE QUARTERDECK LADDER

Showell Styles

A Lythway Book

CHIVERS PRESS
BATH

First published 1982
by
William Kimber & Co Limited
This Large Print edition published by
Chivers Press
by arrangement with
the author
1989

ISBN 0 7451 0913 6

© Showell Styles, 1982

British Library Cataloguing in Publication Data

Styles, Showell, *1908–*
  The quarterdeck ladder.
  I. Title
  823'.914 [F]

ISBN 0-7451-0913-6

All the naval incidents in this story actually took place. Jeremiah Coghlan was a real person and his remarkable career can be traced in Naval records and the Logs of the vessels in which he served.

CONTENTS

1	The Brig *Colombe*	1
2	HMS *Indefatigable*	35
3	Firework Night	75
4	The Rights of Man	110
5	The Dog and The Snake	144
6	Margaret	186
7	Master and Commander	218
	Epilogue	259

CHAPTER ONE

THE BRIG *COLOMBE*

1

Abner Best, master and owner of the smuggling brig *Colombe*, was a prayerful man and not given to swearing, but the oath he muttered into his beard was perhaps excusable. When *Colombe* slipped out of Roscoff harbour with her cargo of illicit brandy the wind had been fair for her homeward run though it was already blowing half a gale. With that westerly she could have followed her usual course, which was northward until she was four leagues off Rame Head and then east-nor'-east for Lulworth; that way she would be far enough from the French coast to disarm the suspicions of any prying Revenue cutter from Poole or Dartmouth. But six hours out of Roscoff the wind had strengthened and veered north-west, causing Captain Best to alter course and double-reef his topsails. And now, with the brig crashing and wallowing through tall green seas, it had veered another point.

'Shapin' for a squaller,' commented Penforth the mate, standing beside Best abaft the two helmsmen. 'Short and nasty, like all such as comes from the Fastnet. She'll not bear her canvas much longer, Abner,' he added, dodging a shower of spray.

Abner Best dashed salt water from his face and nodded. 'Mains and two jibs off her, Sam,' he said briefly.

Penforth jumped for'ard, shouting. 'Hands to take in sail! Main and fore courses, outer and flying jib!'

The hands of the deck-watch squatting below the weather rail scrambled to their feet and ran to the shrouds, headed by a tall youth whose long jet-black hair streamed on the wind. Captain Best watched frowning as the men, dark silhouettes against the grey November sky, swarmed out on the swaying yards to gather and lash the flapping folds of canvas. With his customary northward run no longer possible to him he had two alternatives: to go about and tack far out to westward, losing much ground and delaying the landing of his cargo by a day or more, or to hold on his present course with the Channel Isles and their reefs under his lee.

Knowing his ship and her weatherly qualities, he decided to hold on so long as the gale maintained its present direction. If it veered any more he risked being set on the Casquets or the Grognard or some other of the bristling dangers that defended Guernsey and Alderney, and in that case he would accept it as the Lord's will that he should put about and beat to westward.

'She's a deal easier.' The mate, his tarred-canvas coat streaming water, was back beside him. 'I reckon 'twill blow harder yet, though. Keep they Paimpol sharks in port, maybe.'

Paimpol, like many another French Channel port in this third year of the war with France, had its little fleet of privateers engaged in preying upon the English shipping and pouncing on stragglers from the big convoys. The privateers from Roscoff, where *Colombe* was well-known, were not to be feared, but others would make no distinction between a smuggler and an enemy merchantman.

'We can deal with them,' said Captain Best hardily. 'Just pray the Lord to hold the wind as it is, Sam, and He'll bring us to the Cove at the app'inted hour.'

Whether by reason of the captain's prayers or not, the wind veered no farther. But it blew harder, as Penforth had predicted, rising to a full gale by noon. *Colombe* plunged and swooped among ranks of great white-fanged rollers whose crests seemed to brush the low clouds that raced above them, her masts bare of canvas except for close-reefed topsails and inner jib, her tilted deck swept at intervals by cascades of seawater.

Captain Best sent his mate to organise his small crew into pumping parties and stood by the helm to lend a hand to the two men wrestling with the spokes of the wheel. But the gale endured at this height for no more than two hours, fortunately for the brig. Mid-afternoon brought a rapid drop in the wind's force, and though the grey-green waves marched as mightily as before, heaving the ship skyward and sliding her down into troughs as deep as a Devonshire combe, their crests were no longer blown into flying spray. The continuous clanking of the pumps ceased. The captain, with a curt word to Penforth, went into the little after-cabin that served as a chartroom.

'Tibbs!' Penforth yelled above the noise of wind and sea. 'Foremasthead, and keep your eyes skinned!'

As Tibbs clung his way up the fore-shrouds his shipmates, huddled in their tarpaulins under the rail, discussed the mate's order.

'What's he want with a bloody lookout, this weather?' demanded a thickset man in a fur cap. ''Tis bloody murder at th' masthead when she's rolling thisaway.'

Pegler, a greybearded seaman, shifted and spat. 'He wants what we all want, Mullins—to come safe to Lulworth.'

'Why, no Frog privateer 'd put to sea in this lot,' persisted Mullins, a Hampshire man whose first voyage in *Colombe* this was.

'Cap'n Best will tell ye different, my lad,' said Pegler. 'Right, Jerry?'

'Right,' grunted the black-haired lad squatting beside him.

'Jerry here has been with Cap'n Best more'n six year,' continued Pegler. 'Ship's boy to leading hand, Mullins. He'll tell you as how the cap'n don't do anything without reason. He'll tell you some privateer bastard could be putting out of Jobourg right now to see what the gale's blown in for him. He'll tell you we've made a rare lot of leeway since noon. In yonder—' he jerked his head towards the poop—'Abner Best's calc'lating how far we've been carried southerly. It's my guess the Pleinmont shoals is a scant four leagues on our lee beam this minute, and beyond them there's Alderney—'

'An' the Casquets,' interrupted another of the hands, 'an' the Grognard, same bein' a shoal nigh two mile long—'

'Which is why,' Pegler talked him down firmly, 'we've got young Alf Tibbs at the foremast-head, Mullins. Best eyes in the ship. A reef or a Frog *chasse-marée*, Alf'll spot it, see? You'll learn, Mullins. In the Trade we don't leave aught to chance. 'Tisn't just the gaugers we've to—'

'De-eck there!' The screech from the masthead cut Pegler's lecture short. 'Sail on th' labb'd bow—convoy, headin' west!'

Jeremiah Coghlan shifted his big frame uneasily. Outward-bound convoys were common enough in the Channel in this year of

1796 and he'd seen plenty of them, but they never failed to stir the secret longing in him: a longing that was born in pride and nurtured in shame. No British seaman could fail to feel pride that England, with the three great maritime powers of Europe allied against her, could still—after three years of war—send her merchant ships out past Ushant to the Indies; but few of those who were exempt or had escaped the press-gang were likely to feel shame because they were not serving in the Navy that made this possible. Jeremiah was one of these few. Running brandy across the Channel from Roscoff had its hazards and excitements, evasions and petty skirmishes (all too few for his taste) and the Trade had in six years made a good seaman of him. He liked the life, his ship, and his shipmates. And yet, knowing his country to be in desperate need of men to fight her battles, he was ashamed to be devoting his powers to cheating her—for that, when you reckoned it up, was what smuggling came to. Moreover, these last few years he had been unable to repress an inner conviction that Jeremiah Coghlan was meant for better things than the deck of a brig; though the quarterdeck of a Royal Navy frigate, where in occasional daydreams he saw himself, was far and away beyond possibility.

He sat silent, hunched in his smelly tarpaulin coat on the swaying deck, contemplating these matters while his companions argued about convoy escorts and their duties. Not for a fortune would he have revealed his thoughts to them. Only a madman, they'd tell him, would consider leaving the *Colombe* for a Navy ship. On the one hand short voyages, fresh food, plenty of money to spend ashore; on the other, months or even years at sea, cramped quarters, salt beef and biscuit, flogging and bullying. For only on the lower deck could he enter, and on the lower deck he would stay until he was killed or fell sick and died. Perhaps he was a fool after all, and an ungrateful fool. What would Abner Best say if he knew?

Jeremiah's father, a Polruan fisherman, had died when his son was two years old. His mother was even then a drunkard, with rum the only end and desire of her existence. Abner Best, who had been his father's friend, had taken the lad under his bachelor wing and done for him all that he could, first by paying for his education at Fowey school and later by taking him as ship's boy in his coasting vessels. Natural aptitude and strength beyond the normal had quickly found the youngster a place among the deftest and most knowledgeable seamen, and when Abner acquired the *Colombe* and took to smuggling he made Jeremiah his leading deck-hand.

That Pegler and the other hands accepted his leadership was, as Jeremiah knew, not because of the captain's appointment but because he was unquestionably able to hand, reef, and steer better than any other man aboard; perhaps also (though this he did not know) because he possessed that indefinable and usually inborn quality known as power of command. But to Abner he owed this and other benefits, including the not inconsiderable share of the smuggling profits which paid the rent of the cottage at Polruan and kept his mother supplied with food and (inevitably) rum. Jeremiah Coghlan's square brown face wrinkled in a scowl as he considered all this, and his mouth set itself tightly. Certainly he was an ingrate to think of leaving Abner Best. Henceforth he would eschew impossible daydreams and try to pay back what he owed.

'De-e-eck!' Alf Tibbs's yell from the masthead was urgent. 'Navy cutter headin' from th' convoy—makin' signals, seemin'ly!'

That brought the seamen to their feet and Captain Best out of his chartroom. The convoy to windward was now in sight from the deck when *Colombe* rose on a wavecrest, a huddle of dim grey shapes glimpsed beyond a heaving chaos of mountainous waves. Swooping over the nearer rollers and fast closing the brig came the cutter, riding the green slopes like a seagull under close-reefed fore and mainsail, her command pendant bar-taut on the wind and a wisp of coloured bunting at her yardarm.

'Bugger her signals!' growled Penforth. 'Could be "heave to"—I dunno.'

'If it is he can think again,' said the captain. 'With the way we're making he can speak us easy enough.'

Jeremiah watched with eager admiration as the cutter perfectly handled in the tricky seas, was brought close-hauled within a biscuit-toss of the brig, her black-and-white side displaying six closed gunports as she rose and fell. A young lieutenant hailed from aft.

'What ship's that?'

'Brig *Colombe*,' bellowed the captain. 'Falmouth to Poole with tin ore.'

'Why are you so far off course?'

'Same reason as you—northerly gale,' shouted Best.

The chuckles of his crew at this reply became guffaws a moment later, for the cutter lost her wind in the trough of a huge wave and was forced to turn across the brig's wake. Captain Best went to the poop rail to conduct a further brief exchange with the lieutenant, which Jeremiah was unable to hear, and then the naval craft put about and went swooping back to the convoy. Some minutes later the mate came for'ard to apprise the hands of the news, as was the informal custom aboard *Colombe*.

'Lost one o' the flock—*Upnor Castle*, Indiaman. Main top-mast went by the board in that big blow. If we meet her we're to tell her to put back and wait next convoy.' Penforth spat. 'Bloody impidence, eh? We're not under orders of his commodore.'

'We'll shake out a reef, Sam, main and fore,' called Best from aft.

'Aye, cap'n. Away you go, lads.'

Jeremiah was already away, racing up the main shrouds with Pegler at his heels. His mind as he climbed was full of the trim twelve-gun cutter and her young commander. For him it had been a glimpse of an unattainable heaven, and it was hard to recapture his recent determination not to think of such things. The need for concentration as he edged along the footrope and wrestled with the reef-knots helped him, and by the time he was down on the swaying deck again the cutter was almost forgotten.

Under her extra canvas the brig was better able to make good her course north-eastward, clear by a reasonable margin of the lurking dangers on her lee. But though the gale had moderated the sea had not, and as the stormy afternoon began to darken towards evening *Colombe* was still climbing and falling on mountainous waves that set her stout timbers groaning and kept her helmsmen fully occupied. It was near the end of the afternoon watch when Mullins, who had relieved Tibbs at the foremast-head, hailed the deck to report a rocket fired on the horizon to leeward. A second rocket, a thin bright streak briefly stabbing the lowering clouds, was seen from the deck as the brig rose on a crest.

'Ten to one it's that bloody Indiaman in trouble,' said the mate. 'We can't do anything for her in this sea. And we've a cargo to land,' he added with a covert side-glance at the captain.

Abner Best fingered his beard. 'You've heard of the Good Samaritan, Mr Penforth,' he said severely. 'Would you have me pass by on t'other side? I'll thank you to send the hands to the braces.' He turned to the helmsmen. 'Starboard—handsomely, now. Steady. And meet her quick if she starts to broach.'

The brig heeled as she swung away from the wind and brought it over her larboard quarter, then fled before it like a half-trained hunter, checking in the hollows and surging forward over the crests with the men at the wheel fighting to keep her stern to the waves. A third rocket rose and fell right ahead.

'Bearing sou'-east by east.' Penforth was crouched over the binnacle. 'Three or four mile distant, I'd say.' He straightened himself. 'That'll be about how Alderney bears from us, Abner.'

'Just so, Sam,' returned Captain Best. 'She could have gone on the Grognard.'

'God help her, then.'

'Amen.' Best raised his voice. 'Masthead!

Keep awake!'

Colombe rocked and wallowed onward into the grey gloom. Every man of her little crew was now on deck watching for the next signal from the invisible ship, but no other rockets were seen. It was a long twenty minutes before the hail came from the masthead.

'Wreck—dead ahead!'

Jeremiah Coghlan sprang to the foremast shrouds and ran up them like a cat until he was above the foresail yard. It was a minute or two before he could see anything of the wreck and then it was no more than a glimpse of something black amid the hurrying seas, but when next the brig rose on a wavecrest he saw her plainly, and the sight made him catch his breath. The *Upnor Castle* (it must be she) showed only a narrow strip of her black side, motionless as the invisible shoal that held her on an almost even keel. Fore and main masts had gone by the board and the stump of the mizzen alone remained. Before *Colombe* sank into a trough and the wreck was lost to view he saw a great wave sweep clean across her, beam to beam, so that only the mizzen stump showed above water. That was why there'd been no more distress signals; there could be no one left alive on board the *Upnor Castle*.

But he stayed for another sight of her, though the brig was already reeling and floundering as the helmsmen strove to bring her head-to-wind.

And the clear view he got, brief though it was, showed him the Indiaman's deck that the sea had swept clear amidships of everything that had been on it, including the rail on either beam. It showed him one other thing. At the base of the mizzen stump and in the ragged shrouds that still hung from it there was a compact dark mass, a mass that was rimmed with a fluttering movement as of waving arms.

2

''Tis bloody madness, man!' The mate's voice cracked wildly. 'The best seaman alive couldn't bring a boat alongside her!'

'I've the captain's permission to try, Mr Penforth,' said Jeremiah Coghlan harshly; he swung round. 'Two pair oars in her, extra. Board her, Pegler. Ready with the falls, there—*now*!'

The brig's longboat, with Pegler crouching in her, swayed down from the tackles to the humped crest of a wave. Pegler fended-off while the boat sank in the trough and on the next crest three men swarmed down the falls into her. As Jeremiah straddled the rail Abner Best's hand fell on his shoulder.

'Thirty minutes, lad', he said gruffly.

Jeremiah nodded without looking round and sprang down into the boat, scrambling aft to the sternsheets while Pegler and Bond cast off the falls. The next wave pushed her dangerously close to the rearing flank of the brig but Trevithick in the bows shoved off with a mighty thrust from his oar-loom. Then all four oars were in the rowlocks and furiously pulling her clear. Putting-about (for she had been launched head to wind) was no hazard to men who had spent half their lives in boats, even when the sea was running as high as this; and Jeremiah, when she had spun neatly round on a wave-crest, had little work for his tiller beyond helping his experienced oarsmen to keep her stern-on to the following seas. Pegler, Bond, Trevithick, Hossell—he had called without hesitation for the four best seamen and without hesitation they had stepped forward.

He felt a sudden qualm as he remembered that. For himself, this desperate attempt at rescue was a challenge he had accepted because—well, because it was a challenge. For Abner Best the attempt was a Christian duty. These men, all of them married with families in Looe or Fowey, might well have no such incentives; they might be risking their lives simply because he, Jeremiah Coghlan, had called their names. The thought troubled him sorely, for it was his first realisation of a leader's responsibility. He pushed it resolutely from his mind and fell to considering the action he was about to take, while the longboat drove onward over crest and trough.

Thirty minutes, Abner Best had said. With *Colombe* being carried every moment nearer to the Grognard shoals that was the utmost time her captain could delay. Jeremiah believed the job could be done well within that limit—if it could be done at all. But the light was failing fast. Under the hurrying clouds the seas that shouldered the boat aloft were dark ridges marching towards the invisible shoal. As yet the wreck was invisible too, from this low on the water, but with wind and wave and oars all urging them straight for the *Upnor Castle* there should be a sight of her very soon. Between half-a-mile and a mile to pull, he reckoned.

'We'll take—how many?' grunted Pegler between lusty strokes.

'A score at most.'

Jeremiah groped beneath the stern thwart as he replied, assuring himself that the baler was there on its lanyard. They were likely to need that with the longboat carrying two dozen on her return trip. She was a large boat for a vessel of the brig's tonnage, stoutly built for the ferrying of heavy cargoes of spirits in cask and pulling four oars a side; the spare pairs of oars on her bottom-boards would be manned, he hoped, by four of the survivors from the *Upnor Castle*. It had been impossible to estimate how many were clinging round the stump of the mizzen—certainly only a fraction of her original ship's company—but he thought there might be thirty or forty. Some would have to be left, and there could be no second chance.

His gaze, fixed always ahead, picked out a darker mass in the dark welter of waves as the boat rose on a crest. On the next wave-top Jeremiah stood up, balancing with knee against tiller, and saw the *Upnor Castle* dead ahead and little more than a cable's length away, a mastless hulk with her long deck, tilted slightly towards him, discharging the water left by the wave that had just passed over her. Before the longboat sank into the trough and the wreck was hidden he had seen that there were still living men clustered at the base of the mizzen stump. Above the rush of the wind and the noise of the longboat's progress he heard a shrill chorus of shouts; a chorus that was suddenly overborne by the dull roar of the seas flooding over the Indiaman's deck. How long between waves? Perhaps ten seconds? Twelve? It was hard to say.

'Half a cable to go.' His voice had a natural harshness that made every word emphatic. 'Be ready for orders.'

The wreck in sight again, and nearer. A long wooden wall with the water cascading off it. Penforth had been right when he said no boat could get alongside. Had the captain guessed what he intended? Had the four seamen? He'd told no one because there'd been no time for argument. Now all depended on him.

''Nother minute, lads. Stand by.'

A wild exhilaration rose in him, a surge of power. It was succeeded by a counter-surge of panic as, glancing up from the wave-trough, he saw the dark bar of the Indiaman's side close above. Both passed in a flash and his hand was steady and controlled as he eased the tiller a trifle to starboard so as to head as near that jutting mizzen-stump as he dared.

'We're going aboard her. Lug 'em inboard as they come. Count twenty, Pegler. Fend off the rest.'

No word came from the men toiling at the oars and Jeremiah did not look at them. All his attention was fixed on the watery slope above the longboat's bow, receding and seeming to sink as the succeeding wave began to lift her stern. The long flank of the wreck loomed like a cliff almost overhead and vanished again. Beneath him he felt the mighty upsurge of the wave.

'Pull! *Pull!*'

The boat rose, rising the smooth crest. Very close now was the jagged pillar of the mizzen, loud in his ears the roar of waves beyond. *Upnor Castle*'s deck planking seemed to rush towards him—they would surely be swept clean over the wreck.

'*Back together!*'

As he gave the order he knew the futility of

that effort against the tremendous force that flung her forward. But the wave slowed from its own impact, and amid a seething turmoil of subsiding water the longboat crashed and slid onto the Indiaman's deck, lurching to a halt twenty feet from the mizzen-stump. Then came chaos.

Through the shallow back-rush of water a throng of dark figures hurled themselves at the boat, screeching and shoving. Pegler and his mates dragged them in over the gunwale while others of the survivors fought to oust those who had been foremost in the rush. Something that looked like a bale of cloth clutched with skinny hands at Jeremiah's coat and was plucked from its hold by a big seaman who got a leg over the gunwale. Jeremiah swung his fist savagely and the man flew backwards. He lugged the cloth-wrapped figure onto the bottom-boards, shot a glance at the already crowded space between the thwarts, kicked mercilessly at a man who was trying to roll himself inboard over the stern. He felt rather than saw the loom of the oncoming wave.

'Man those oars! Get—'

He fell sprawling across the stern thwart as the longboat was picked up and hurled like a stone from a sling. The thwart tilted and spun under him and water splashed across his face, and for an instant he thought she had capsized. Then, somehow, he was right-side-up and clutching the tiller, while the boat pitched and tossed and rolled through a waste of confused waves quite different from the surging rollers that had borne her onto the *Upnor Castle*'s deck.

Jeremiah, collecting his scattered wits, realised that they were under the lee of the Indiaman's half-submerged hull, with shoal water beneath the longboat's bottom. Of the Grognard he knew nothing save that at its seaward edge where the ship had run upon it there must be less than five fathoms. He must go about now or risk being carried onto the reefs that might lie only a little way to leeward. So crowded was the boat that at first glance she seemed a disorderly huddle of men incapable of action, but then he saw that at least the spare oars had been manned and she could pull four a side.

'Get down, there—down on the bottomboards!' he yelled. 'Starboard oars, pull! Again—now give way together!'

The wind gusting between the toppling waves was on his left cheek and the boat was lurching awkwardly through the welter, heading to clear the vicinity of the wreck. Jeremiah became aware of the water swilling round his ankles. Reaching for the baler, he thrust it into the hand of a man who was huddled against his knees.

'Here—bale for your life!' He stood up.

'Trim the boat, for'ard there. And keep still.'

A quick look round him before he sat down showed him the wreck's position, visible only by the spouts of white water, half-a-cable away on the larboard quarter. The longboat was rolling in the troughs of taller and sleeker waves. He used the tiller to bring her bows-on to the advancing rollers and she began to climb and fall with a steady progress into the eye of the wind, heading back to the brig. It would be a hard pull, even though (as he now saw) Pegler had double-banked the oars on the midships thwarts, but the danger was past. The job was done.

With that realisation came quick reaction. In the period of stress and action since they had put off from the brig Jeremiah had been conscious of no physical feeling at all. Now, of a sudden, he was shivering with the cold of the wind and his wet clothing, aware of the pain of split knuckles. Remembering the man he had hit, he felt sick at the thought that his blow had doomed that man to death. The grey twilight darkening over the black marching ranks of the waves seemed imexpressibly melancholy, and for a moment he was near to bursting into tears.

'We got eighteen.' Pegler's voice came above the creak and splash of the oars. 'Was nineteen,' it added, 'but one bugger fell overboard.'

From a tendency to weep Jeremiah veered to

a hysterical desire to laugh. *One bugger fell overboard.* In Pegler's rich Devon tones the statement struck him as comical. Then the moment of irrationality passed and he was himself again, aware of cold and pain but able to ignore them, aware of the heaving seas and the longboat's scant twelve inches of freeboard; aware also that he and his shipmates had saved eighteen lives.

It was as well that they had taken aboard no more—the longboat was laden to capacity, all the space between the thwarts packed with crouching or recumbent survivors, some of them apparently insensible (which was hardly remarkable after their ordeal) and one or two talking loudly. When the longboat rose on the next crest he saw the *Colombe* much nearer than he had expected. Jeremiah stood up and waved his arm, and the sound of a ragged cheer came down the wind. Captain Best had rigged a scrambling-net along her side, he noted, and shaken the reefs from her topsails.

'Five minutes more and we'll be alongside,' he announced cheerfully as he sat down.

It was *Colombe*'s drifting downwind that had shortened the return journey, of course. Abner Best must have been on tenterhooks for the safety of his ship. Jeremiah tried to estimate how long the boat had been away from her and found it impossible; time had stood still for him through all that period. A queer thing, that, a man's sense of time and his bodily senses being stolen from him during a spell of action—after it too, for he'd never noticed that the baling had stopped and the longboat was dry, or that his right foot was resting on a bundle of cloth.

The bundle moved and a cracked voice spoke.

'You'll obleege, young man, by taking your boot from my neck.'

Jeremiah hastily removed his foot. The bundle, he saw, was a little old woman swathed in cloaks; but before he could make apology his eye caught the wet gleam of the brig's side very close ahead and he was instantly occupied with the tricky business of bringing the boat alongside.

It was no easy operation to hoist eighteen persons, half of them little better than helpless, from the tossing longboat into the heaving brig, but it was accomplished speedily and safely. They were supported below to be wrapped in blankets and dosed with brandy, except for the old lady who was installed in Captain Best's little sleeping-cabin. Jeremiah, last out of the boat, had received characteristic welcomes from mate and captain; from Penforth the heartfelt assertion that he was bloody lucky to be alive, from Abner Best the expressed conviction that the Lord had been with him and so powerful a clasp of Jeremiah's damaged hand that he barely stifled his yell of pain. He was later to learn from Penforth, who had watched the rescue attempt through his glass, that the wave that had lifted the longboat from the wreck had left no one alive on the deck of the *Upnor Castle*.

It was at two bells of the first watch, *Colombe* having cleared all dangers and made good progress on her northerly course, that Captain Best softly opened the door of his sleeping-cabin and endeavoured, by the light of a candle-lantern, to see that all was well with its occupant. A pair of sharp little eyes blinked at him.

'Come in and shut the door, man,' said the old lady as one accustomed to command. 'I'm not afraid of gossip.'

Abner Best blushed and obeyed. From the folds of a blanket her small wrinkled face regarded him amusedly.

'You've my heartfelt gratitude for your aid, captain,' she said. 'Also for a dram of the best cognac I've ever tasted. You've a deal more of it on board, I dare say.' She gave a crackle of a laugh at his embarrassment. 'Never fear—I'll not tell the Revenue. And my thanks are sincere, sir.'

''Twas the Lord's doing, ma'am—thank Him,' said Abner, improving the occasion.

'I do. But there was a young man who did the Lord's work for him. I want to know his name.'

'Jeremiah Coghlan, ma'am.'

'Indeed. Well, I'm Lady Tyler and I shall see that Jeremiah Coghlan is not forgotten. Now, if you please, go away.'

3

Captain Best discovered that Good Samaritans can suffer for their Samaritanism. He had accepted with Christian resignation the delay in landing his cargo at Lulworth Cove, but within twenty-four hours it had become probable that he would lose his brandy-casks and more besides.

During the night that followed the rescue it became clear that one of the *Upnor Castle* survivors was so gravely ill that it behoved the captain to put into the nearest port, where the man could receive the care that would give him a chance of life. At daybreak, the wind having moderated and backed southerly, he set the brig on a course for Plymouth, abandoning his plan of putting his passengers off at Exmouth which was more than twice as far. *Colombe* sailed into Cawsand Bay, passing a big frigate anchored there which Penforth identified as Sir Edward Pellew's *Indefatigable*, and dropped anchor a little before noon on November 12th within gunshot of Drake's Island.

The authorities on shore acted promptly as soon as the news reached them. The survivors were taken off in boats, the sick man to go to hospital and the others to houses where they would be looked after until they could be returned to their homes. Sir Edward Pellew, who was ashore while *Indefatigable* revictualled, sent his carriage to convey Lady Tyler to his house on Citadel Hill; and as Jeremiah Coghlan was at this time absent from the brig on matters of business she was unable to thank her rescuer personally. She had been on her way in *Upnor Castle* to join her husband, who was Deputy Governor in Barbados.

And now Abner Best was in a tight corner. The necessary reports and statements concerning the Indiaman and the circumstances of the rescue would keep him here for two or three days at the least, while his brig lay amid the bustle of the harbour with her hold full of smuggled brandy. Plymouth was one of the few South Coast ports where Captain Best had no comfortable arrangement with the local Revenue Office. He had sent Penforth and Coghlan ashore at the first opportunity, to seek out someone among the smuggling fraternity who might help him; the name of a venial Revenue officer could lead to negotiations and eventual safety. But in the meantime a Revenue inspection—and nothing was more likely—would certainly result in the confiscation of his cargo and the imprisonment of himself and his crew in Plymouth jail pending their trial. A further worry was that he could not decide whether or not he should pray for the Lord's help on such a matter.

The investigations ashore bore no fruit on the first day. In the early forenoon of the second, before Jeremiah and the mate left the ship, a boat pulled out of the sea-fog that lay across the harbour to deliver a letter addressed to Jeremiah Coghlan. The dripping blanket of the fog took on a sudden brightness as Jeremiah read the bold angular scrawl.

Sir,
    Lady Tyler presently my guest has described to me yr. Gallant and Seaman-like conduct on 11th November. In the result I cannot but feel yr. Services would be of notable Value in His Majesty's Navy. Indefatigable sails the afternoon Tide of the 16th the Wind being fair. Should you care to join I shall be on board the 15th and you may report to me at Noon of that day. Provided yr. Sea Time allows it you will be made Midshipman and may be assured of my further Patronage.
                              EDWARD PELLEW, *Bart.*
Post Scriptum. Pray inform the Master of the Colombe *brig I have represented to the Port Admiral that no Inspection shall be made of his Cargo.*

Jeremiah read this letter a second time; and

then, more slowly, a third time. The brightness faded. He crossed the deck to the chartroom where the captain was conning his accounts and laid the letter on the desk before him without a word. Abner Best adjusted the steel-rimmed spectacles he wore for close work and studied Pellew's letter with care. There was a longish pause before he sat back and pushed the spectacles up on his brow to stare at his leading hand.

'You can belay the trip ashore,' he said. 'Tell Mr Penforth. The Lord protects his own,' he added complacently.

'Aye, cap'n,' said Jeremiah. 'And—for the rest of it?'

'You'll do as Sir Ed'ard says, of course.'

'I shall stay with you. I'm resolved to—'

'You're resolved to fly in the face of Providence!' The captain, with an unusual display of emotion, banged his fist on the table. 'Well, I'm resolved you shan't, my lad. Sir Ed'ard's the finest sea-officer in the Navy and a Cornishman to boot. I know what you want,' he added more gently, 'and this is the only chance of it you'll get.'

'But—'

'The longboat can put you aboard *Indefatigable* on the fifteenth. You've shore leave from now till nightfall tomorrow to take leave of your mother—and anybody else.' Abner's bearded face wore one of its rare smiles as he spoke. 'And now I'll thank you to leave me to my accounts,' he ended gruffly.

Out on deck there was brightness again, to Jeremiah Coghlan's inner eye at least; the prospect of glory and promotion was not less dazzling for the suddenness with which it had come upon him. In actuality the fog continued to hang darkly above the waters of harbour and Sound with no breeze to shift it, and there was not a single craft to be found to take him along the coast to Polruan or even as far as Looe. When he was not on board *Colombe* Jeremiah had a room in Abner Best's house at Bridport and he dreaded the rare visits to his mother's cottage. He would gladly have shirked this one. Polruan was thirty miles by road from Plymouth and it was just conceivable that some unforeseen chance might prevent his punctual appearance on board *Indefatigable*. But Abner had taken care to imbue him with a proper sense of filial duty and there was no knowing when he would see his mother again. Besides, he needed to say his farewells to Susan Cargis.

He found a carrier's cart going to Looe and reached that place after a slow journey on bad roads. Discovering that the carrier was returning next day, leaving Looe at noon, Jeremiah was able to secure his line of retreat with a fee in advance and set out to walk the rest of the way. The fog had given place to a thin rain as he crossed over to West Looe and trudged up the steep muddy lane that led across the hills, the November twilight was gathering, and he had a nine-mile walk before him, but he knew every yard of the way and the knowledge of what awaited him at the end of it could not lower his high spirits.

He was, he told himself, on the high road to fortune. In no very great number of years he could be driving in his own carriage, calling on the Paddons up at the Hall, when he came ashore; walking the quarterdeck of a 74 when he was at sea. All that upper world of gentry and nobility had been inaccessible to him except by the one step—very rarely offered—which Sir Edward Pellew was to give him: the step up to the quarterdeck. Even that was only the lowest rung of a ladder. But once his foot was on it he could climb: lieutenant, master and commander, post captain at last, perhaps. And once he was made post nothing save death could prevent him from becoming an admiral. The muddy miles fell behind him almost unnoticed with such matters to occupy his thoughts. The big farmhouse of Trevarder, Susan's home and less than three miles from Polruan, took him by surprise when he saw its black bulk and single lit window beyond the fork of narrow lanes.

Tom Cargis, the farmer, opened to him and greeted him warmly. Susan and her ma were from home, gone to stay for a week at Liskeard with Mrs Cargis's sister—but Jeremiah would come in for a bite and a sup, surely? Jeremiah, knowing there would be nothing for him at his mother's, spent half-an-hour with Tom over bread-and-cheese and cider and then set forth again into the darkness.

The drizzle had stopped. The hidden moon, nearing its last quarter, gave a feeble luminosity to the clouds and in a field a quarter of a mile past Trevarder Jeremiah could just make out the barn where he and Susan had made love—his first proper lovemaking. Fortunately nothing awkward had come of it, but he had promised then to marry Susan some day and that promise he would keep. She was a hearty, handsome lass, as old as he and nearly as tall, and would make a wife to be proud of when—and there he came to a stop in sudden doubt. Susan might do very well for Jeremiah Coghlan, seaman and smuggler, but what sort of wife went with Captain Coghlan—Captain Sir Jeremiah Coghlan, come to that?

Uneasy reflections on this theme occupied him while he trudged round the rim of Lantic Bay, with the murmur of an invisible surf far down on his left hand; but the sight of Fowey's sprinkle of lights across the dark gulf of the river sent them from his head, driven out by the beginnings of a familiar revulsion. When the track started to zigzag down past the first cottages of Polruan he was consciously bracing himself for the coming meeting.

Steep and slippery cobblestones shone wetly in the splash of light from the inn window, whence also poured a cheerful clamour of voices. Mrs Coghlan no longer spent her evenings at the inn; better for her, perhaps, if she did. He passed the inn and saw the glimmer of Fowey river below the hard where the black shapes of boats lay like animals asleep. A pavement of uneven stone slabs on the left took him along the front of a row of whitewashed cottages, at the fourth of which he halted. Dim candlelight illumined a dirty window and broken glass crunched beneath his boot as he stepped to the door and knocked on it. It swung open under his hand and he went in.

The reek of spirits came at him like a blow in the face. The little bow-beamed room was stuffy with the heat from a driftwood fire and smelt of dirt as well as of rum. Mary Coghlan was sprawled on a broken-down couch near the fire, with a full glass and a half-empty bottle on the low table within reach. She wore a soiled pink gown unbuttoned at the breast, and the untidy mass of greying blond hair was pulled across her face so that Jeremiah could not tell whether she was asleep or awake.

'Mother,' he said loudly. 'It's Jeremiah.'

She made an inarticulate sound and turned her head, pushing her hair aside with a shaking hand. It was just possible to discern that she had once been beautiful, that the large blue eyes—red-rimmed and watery now—had once looked from a face that must have turned many a man's head to look at her. Little was left of that youthful ghost in the flaccid cheeks, blotched and mottled, and the loose mouth hanging open and awry with a dribble of moisture at the corner. She had no greeting for him and her gaze wandered aside from his. Jeremiah saw that she was far gone in drink. He went to stand beside the table, looking down at her, miserably conscious of his own shortcomings. But what could he have done, as a little boy, to prevent this? And what could he do now?

'Mother,' he said, speaking slowly and clearly, 'I've come to say goodbye for a while. I've had a piece of good fortune. Sir Edward—'

'You've brought my money?' Her speech was so slurred that only the avid gleam in her eyes made the words intelligible to him.

'All I've got, mother.'

He emptied his pockets onto the table, careful to display the lining of each pocket. Abner Best had paid over Jeremiah's share of the *Colombe*'s profits to date and the thirteen guineas was only half the sum he had received, so he was deceiving her; but knowledge of the use she would make of it, and of his own future needs, blunted his conscience. His mother reached trembling hands for the gold and would have knocked it to the floor if he hadn't reached a mug from the dresser and put the coins into it.

'I'm joining *Indefatigable*, day after tomorrow,' he told her, trying to reach her understanding. 'I'm to be midshipman in a King's ship.'

Her gaze shifted slowly from the money to his face but it held no sign of comprehension.

'A midshipman,' he repeated more loudly. 'On the quarterdeck of a King's ship, mother.'

A gleam of intelligence came into the watery eyes and she seemed to rouse herself with an effort.

'The quarterdeck.' The words were quite distinct now. 'Right place for my son. Right place for his father. Right place—'

Her voice wavered and faded. She stretched a hand for the glass of rum; and Jeremiah, thinking to take advantage of this more lucid moment, quickly covered her hand with his own.

'Mother, listen to me,' he said urgently. 'This stuff's killing you. For your own sake, for my sake too, try to—'

With a bestial sound that was half screech and half snarl she snatched her hand clear and clutched the glass, spilling half the contents as she tossed them down her throat. Then she loosed drunken fury at him in a torrent of curses, her face crimson and working with rage, the filthy words tumbling over each other and mostly incomprehensible. The outburst ceased suddenly and she fell back as if she had been knocked down.

Her son stood motionless and frowning for a few moments. The morning might find her less disordered—but he couldn't stay here; the place sickened him. He went to the fire and pushed the smouldering sticks back from the hearth, blocking them safely into the fireplace with the stone kerb. His mother was unconscious, snoring. He bent over her and kissed the mottled cheek. Then he went out, latching the door behind him.

The night seemed darker than before and the thin rain had begun again. He turned up the lane past the inn—they were singing a discordant chantey behind that lamplit window—and trudged on uphill and away from Polruan. To ease the sickness at his heart he tried to recapture the inner brightness of the morning, willing himself to recognise his wonderful good fortune. He was to sail with Edward Pellew, famed as the first sea-officer of the day, knighted for that triumphant single-ship action with *Cléopatre*, made baronet after the epic rescue of the whole ship's company of a stranded transport. He was to have a place, humble enough but still a place, on the quarterdeck of a fighting frigate. *Right place for my son.* Jeremiah could agree with his mother there; when she had added *Right place for his father* she must have been mazed by rum, for he had always heard that William Coghlan was a humble man and illiterate, though a fair hand with a fishing-boat.

His thoughts had taken him back to the scene he had just left and he couldn't shift them to the visionary future. He was a poor fisherman's son with a drunken slut of a mother. He shut his mind (he had been able to do this since his schooldays) to everything except the immediate objective, which was shelter and dry straw.

Thirty minutes of trudging through darkness and rain brought him to the field-gate. He crossed the stubble to the barn where he and Susan had lain together, groped his way in and found the baled straw, and lay down to sleep in his wet clothes.

CHAPTER TWO

HMS *INDEFATIGABLE*

1

Captain Sir Edward Pellew sat at his table in *Indefatigable*'s stern cabin below the quarterdeck, his red brows bent as he scrutinised the frigate's repair list. Beside him Thomson, his burly first lieutenant, pointed out the replacements which Plymouth dockyard had been unable to supply in the short time at their disposal. From the upper deck outside came a ceaseless hubbub of noise—a mingling of shouts, thuds, and the rattle of blocks and tackles—as the ship prepared for sea. Though it was midday the stern windows admitted only a gloomy light, for a sou'wester was driving a dark rain-squall up the Sound below the scowling November sky.

It was a roomy cabin for a frigate and had indeed been the ship's state-room. *Indefatigable* was a *razée*, a 64-gun battleship cut down by one deck to increase her speed and ease of manoeuvring, and she was the darling of Pellew's heart. He had fought a hard battle with Admiralty to retain her tall masts at their original height and arm her according to his own ideas of fighting efficiency, and now her forty-four guns and vast spread of canvas made her as formidable as the best of the big frigates the French had lately been building. He had commanded her for a year, and in that time his infectious enthusiasm, coupled with a stern justice that made no exceptions, had made seamen of the landsmen and jailbirds who had formed threequarters of her original crew.

Four double clangs from the belfry above the cabin indicated noon, eight bells of the forenoon watch. Pellew nodded resignedly and handed the list to the first lieutenant.

'She'll do,' he said. 'You've done well to accomplish so much, Mr Thomson.'

'Thankee, sir,' said Thomson, beaming.

There was a metallic clash outside the cabin door as the marine sentry on duty there came to attention. George Bell, fourth lieutenant, put his head into the cabin.

'If you please, sir—I've a man here, Coghlan by name, just come aboard. Says he has orders to report to you at noon.'

'So he has,' nodded Pellew. 'Send him in. And send Mr Benedict aft here.—Thank you, Mr Thomson. I'll see that new t'gallant yard when you have it rigged.'

As he left the cabin Thomson narrowly avoided collision with a tall fellow ducking his head to enter. Jeremiah Coghlan would have liked to bear himself erect before his future commander, but though *Indefatigable*'s stern cabin boasted nearly six feet of headroom he was forced to stand with his chin on his chest and his shoulders hunched, uncomfortably aware of the hangdog effect this must produce. Sir Edward had turned aside to stuff some papers into a chest by his chair. He was a big man, Jeremiah saw, nigh as tall as himself by the look of him, with reddish hair turning grey. A tight obstinate mouth and a grim jaw—

Sir Edward swung round and their eyes met. The captain's widened and his heavy brows met in a sudden frown. Jeremiah, conscious of the ill-fitting white breeches and blue coat he had bought at the Plymouth slop-merchant's (a proper midshipman's rig, he had been told), blushed and tried to straighten the folds of his breeches without being seen to do so. His embarrassment was evidently perceived. Sir Edward lowered his gaze and cleared his throat loudly. The hint of a smile that appeared at the corner of his mouth transformed his grimness to benevolence.

'Your pardon,' he said, harsh-voiced but courteous. 'You've something the look of an old acquaintance of mine, long dead. Well. Mr Jeremiah Coghlan, I believe?'

'Yes, Sir Edward.'

'I'm Sir Edward to their Lordships—and to my chaplain, can't break him out of it—but you'll call me "sir", Mr Coghlan. Remember that.'

'Aye, aye, sir.'

Pellew's eyes twinkled. They were brown, Jeremiah saw, not blue or grey as one might have expected in that lean weather-beaten face, and with that colouring.

'You've learned your responses, I see,' said Pellew. 'That's to be expected.' He ran his glance over Jeremiah's clothes from buckled shoes to carefully-tied stock. 'You've still to learn not to rush your fences. You're not yet rated midshipman, Mr Coghlan.'

Jeremiah blushed again. 'No, sir.'

'Don't take anything for granted. It never pays. What sea-time can you claim?'

'Seven years, sir, bar one month. Cap'n Best gave me this certificate—'

'Never mind.' Pellew waved the paper away. 'I shall rate you midshipman from noon today—come in, Mr Benedict.' A studious-looking youth with lank fair hair advanced to the table. 'Show Mr Coghlan his quarters. See that he knows his duties, and his way round the ship, before tomorrow. Mr Benedict is my senior midshipman,' he added to Jeremiah. 'Now carry on, both of you.'

'Aye aye, sir,' said Benedict; he nudged the new midshipman's arm and they turned together towards the door.

'Mr Coghlan!' Pellew's voice arrested them. 'Where were you born?'

'Polruan, sir.'

'Polruan,' replied Pellew thoughtfully. 'Yes. Well—carry on.'

Jeremiah followed the senior midshipman out into the noise and activity of the upper deck, where a swarm of men, bare-footed on the rain-wet planking, were trundling away the beef-casks that had just been swayed aboard on the tackles. If Pellew's odd reaction to his appearance puzzled him it was only for a moment, for he was bracing himself for an ordeal far more trying than his interview with *Indefatigable*'s captain. He had never trodden the decks of a King's ship before this day, but from the gossip of the ports and the tavern yarns of men-of-war's men he had picked up what he conceived to be a true idea of the Navy's peculiarities. Sir Edward Pellew, it was true, had not quite conformed to the usual pattern (as reported in the taverns) of a tyrannical despot, but Jeremiah fully expected to find the midshipmen's berth inhabited by young gentlemen of quality whose prime amusement was to bully and castigate the lower orders. In a famous frigate commanded by a baronet these fledgling officers were likely to be all sprigs of the nobility. How would they receive the news that a Polruan fisherman's son had come to live among them? Jeremiah bristled with anticipatory resentment of the whips and scorns that would surely be his lot.

'Where's your dunnage?' demanded Benedict, halting suddenly at the after-hatch.

'By the entry port. It's a sea-chest.'

'Come on, then. I'll lend a hand.' Benedict dodged a way through the cask-trundlers. 'You could order a couple of hands to bring it below but they've got enough to do.'

He took the rope handle at one end of the chest, Jeremiah took the other, and they zigzagged back through the throng to the after-hatch. Manhandling the chest down two steep ladders in semi-darkness was no easy task, and Benedict was breathing hard when they reached the bottom.

'Orlop deck,' he panted. 'Our berth's—the cockpit, yonder.'

Down here in the blackness of the 'tween-decks the great wooden shell of the hull echoed and vibrated to the sounds of continuous activity as *Indefatigable*'s hold received the stores for her voyage. A glow of light at the side of the alleyway a few yards away came from the cockpit, as Jeremiah saw when Benedict steered him and his sea-chest in through a narrow opening. A horn lantern suspended from the deckhead threw a sombre light on the red-painted table that occupied most of the space in the small wooden-walled room. Three young men, one of them little more than a boy, sat at the table eating bread and cheese and drinking wine out of tin mugs.

'Here's the neophyte, gentlemen,' said Benedict, lowering the chest to the deck. 'Mr Coghlan—Mr Caldecott, Mr Delamere, Mr Paddon. Mr Paddon,' he added to Jeremiah, 'rates officer's servant and has yet to attain our lofty rank.'

'Pray forgive us if we don't rise and bow,' said Delamere, a thickset lad in shirtsleeves with loosened stock. 'There's just five foot of headroom in this bloody place.'

Caldecott reached a mug and platter from the shelf behind him without rising from his bench. His long solemn face was flanked by protruding ears.

'You find us taking a noon bever, Mr Coghlan,' he said. 'Be seated rather than bent double as at present, and join us. This is Ducky's mug but he's on gangway duty.'

He poured wine into the mug and pushed it across the table. Benedict and Jeremiah sat down.

'Ducky is Mr FitzJames,' Benedict explained. 'He gets called that because his uncle's a Duke.' He helped himself to cheese. 'We'd best leave the poor lad a crumb for when he comes off duty.'

'By God you shock me, Ben!' Delamere said. 'A crumb, forsooth! It would be an exact sixth according to your damned egalitarian notions. Where are your Rights of Man, eh?'

'Ben's a Jacobin,' said Caldecott. 'He wants to grind the faces of the aristos. One crumb for Duke's nephew, two for the Hon John Delamere, three for Charles Paddon of Trenythan, but good large hunks for commoners like himself and poor Georgie Caldecott.'

'I deny it,' Benedict said tranquilly. 'But it's a good idea all the same. As mess president I'll consider it.'

This brought a duet of chaffing protest from Caldecott and Delamere to which Jeremiah didn't listen. He was telling himself gloomily that his worst fears were realised. He had not

42

fully understood his companions' badinage but he had learned from it that at least three of his future messmates came from the titled upper classes; FitzJames (whom he had seen on duty at the entry port) was the nephew of a Duke, Delamere was an Honourable which meant he was the son of a lord, and Paddon—as he had known when he heard his name—was the son of Lady Paddon of Trenythan Hall above Fowey. And Benedict and Caldecott were gentry, no doubt of that. They seemed pleasant fellows enough, but they'd yet to discover his lowly origins. And the sooner that was over with the better.

'Anyway,' Benedict was saying, 'if I'm an egalitarian I'm not an international one. I'll maintain that one Briton can beat any three Frenchmen, and one Hampshire man—which is me—can beat any four. Mr Coghlan's a Cornishman, by the bye,' he added.

'Indeed?' said young Paddon, speaking for the first time. 'Then that makes two of us, Mr Coghlan.'

He was a slightly-built youngster, dark-haired and handsome. Jeremiah knew that Lady Paddon was a widow and that she had twin children, a boy and a girl; that was common knowledge when he was a lad at Fowey school, for the Hall was only a mile or two from Fowey, and Sir John Paddon, when he was alive, had been the squire. This lad of sixteen or seventeen wasn't Sir Charles, because his father had been a plain knight of the shire, but with his finely-chiselled features and air of aloofness he looked much more the young lord than any of the others.

'I thought I knew most of our Cornish families,' Paddon said in his drawling voice, 'but I cannot just now recall the Coghlans. What part of the Duchy do you hail from, sir?'

This was the moment. Jeremiah drew a deep breath.

'I come from Polruan,' he said. 'My father was a poor fisherman, Mr Paddon.'

He knew as soon as he had spoken that his harsh voice had been too loud, that he had contrived to sound aggressively defiant, but it was too late now. He set his jaw and sat scowling at the table, aware that an awkward silence had fallen. Delamere grimaced and scratched his neck. Caldecott raised his brows and looked at Benedict. Benedict cleared his throat loudly and spoke.

'Mr Coghlan,' he said reprovingly, 'you had better understand once for all that in *Indefatigable*—I say nothing of other ships—we attach more importance to what a man does than to who he is. We—'

'That's a crib,' interrupted Delamere. 'Red Ned said that to me when I joined, word for word.'

'Have the goodness to pipe down, sir!'

Benedict was genuinely angry and Delamere looked abashed. 'To resume, Mr Coghlan,' he continued in his somewhat pedantic tone, 'we judge every man by the way he does his duty in his own particular rank or rating. It's a new kind of social order in a King's ship. A man works for the ship instead of for himself—it's all planned for the ship and the ship's planned to fight the French. There's no room for idlers as there is on shore, nor for the wealthy aristocrat who contributes nothing to the State—'

'My God! Here we go again,' muttered Delamere.

'In short, Mr Coghlan,' Caldecott said quickly, forestalling an outburst from the orator, 'if you're a midshipman of *Indefatigable* nobody—except yourself, of course—cares who your father was.'

'In fact,' said Delamere, 'we're all bastards when the first lieutenant gives us a rough-tonguing.'

'What with that and sermons from the senior mid,' said Caldecott, 'our life ain't worth living.'

'Ben would have made a bloody good parson,' Delamere added.

Jeremiah, conscious that his face was very red, knew that they were trying to help his embarrassment. He sought for the right words and found them.

'Mr Benedict's latest sermon made one convert, at any rate,' he said quietly. 'I confess my sin and hope to be forgiven.'

Delamere grinned and nodded approvingly. Caldecott pulled a long face and rolled his eyes heavenward.

'Let us give thanks,' he intoned, 'for a brand plucked from the burning. Nevertheless, brother, we shall lay a penance upon you. You shall—'

He stopped as a short round-faced midshipman burst abruptly into the cabin. Mr FitzJames tossed hat and dirk on the table and spoke breathlessly.

'First lieutenant's compliments and why the hell aren't the young gentlemen on deck?'

'Christ!' Benedict scrambled to his feet. 'On deck, all, and look lively. You'd better stick with me, Coghlan—bosun's working-party for'ard. Paddon, clear away here when Ducky's finished.'

He grabbed his hat, Jeremiah grabbed his, and they clattered up the ladders after the other two midshipmen.

2

Indefatigable sailed in the afternoon of the following day, beating out of Cawsand Bay in a westerly gale under courses and topsails. She was returning to her station off the Biscay coast. Following the centuries-old custom, Admiral Lord Bridport had taken his main Channel Fleet into Portsmouth for the winter, leaving Sir John Colpoys with ten sail of the line and four frigates to blockade the enemy line-of-battle ships in Brest and L'Orient and Rochefort. Pellew and the rest of his little squadron—*Revolutionnaire, Amazon* and *Phoebe*—had the task of keeping close watch on the French naval concentration, which Sir Edward believed to indicate an imminent attempt to break through the weakened British cordon. This and a great deal more Mr Midshipman Jeremiah Coghlan learned in the twenty-four hours before *Indefatigable* upped anchor.

About seamanship in the broad sense Jeremiah had little to learn. He could hand, reef, and steer with any man, and sheets and halyards and the diversities of a square-rigged vessel's cordage had no secrets from him. It was the Navy way of dealing with these things, the rigid method, the irrefrangible rule, that had to be assimilated. Since he was resolute to learn and quick of perception he made few mistakes and never the same one twice. This was just as well, for a mistake—like any other crime tending to undermine the ship's fighting efficiency—brought swift punishment on board *Indefatigable*.

Before the frigate made her landfall off Ushant Jeremiah had suffered a blistering from the first lieutenant's tongue and spent a rain-drenched forenoon watch at the masthead by order of Mr Gaze, the second, for failing to report a frayed relieving-tackle on number nine gun upper-deck, one of the two allotted to his charge. But that was the extent of his sufferings under naval discipline, and though he saw the bosuns' colts used with a will on the buttocks of laggardly seamen no one but the laggards appeared to find this unsatisfactory. He saw his first flogging, however, before the frigate had been twenty-four hours at sea.

At noon of the second day, the wind having veered to the northward and moderated, the order was piped and shouted—'Hands to witness punishment!'—and every soul on board with the exception of those occupied with the sailing of the ship came aft at the double. The two dozen red-coated marines (it was the first time Jeremiah had seen them) clattered up to the poop with their muskets and sidearms, the seamen formed a rough hollow-square aft of the mizzen-mast, and Captain Pellew and his lieutenants appeared on the weather side of the quarter-deck. Jeremiah and his fellow midshipmen gathered under the break of the poop. It was all done with phenomenal swiftness and the silence that fell when the shuffle of feet had ceased was impressive.

'Rig the gratings!' Pellew ordered, his voice harsh and clear above the shrilling of wind in the cordage.

In a twinkling one of the heavy square hatch-gratings was reared against the for'ard edge of the poop deck and another laid flat in front of it. The master-at-arms brought forward the offender, a pigtailed seaman clad in shirt and trousers.

'Tom Cattermole,' said Pellew incisively, 'your offence is proven. Drunk on watch. You know the penalty. Anything to say?'

'No, sir.'

'Strip, then.'

The seaman pulled off his shirt and the master-at-arms took it from him. Pellew took off his hat (every man who was covered at once did the same) and opened the tattered book he had been carrying under his arm.

'Seize him up,' he snapped, and began to read aloud, very rapidly, that one of the Articles of War relevant to Tom Cattermole's offence. Jeremiah heard him with half an ear; his attention was fixed on the prisoner, who walked quickly—but with a studied nonchalance all the same—to the gratings to stand with his arms extended against the upright and his naked back to the assembly. Two quartermasters tied his wrists to the grating with spunyarn while a bosun's mate stood forward with the red-painted cat, drawing through his fingers the nine two-foot cords. Pellew finished his reading and clapped his hat on his head.

'Do your duty, Barratt,' he said loudly.

The bosun's mate positioned himself with some ceremony and swung his outstretched right arm back slowly. At the first blow, which raised a skein of thin red lines on the bare skin, Cattermole neither flinched nor cried out. The second and third made him cringe and give an inarticulate cry, but three more lashes fell without wringing a sound from him though his body writhed and cringed. The sixth stroke was the last. By now blood from back and shoulders was dripping on the grating, but the seaman stood upright when his wrists were freed and contrived to sling his shirt about him without wincing. Two of his messmates came forward to help him below and the throng of watching men parted silently to let them through.

'You can dismiss all hands, Mr Thomson,' said Pellew, turning away.

Thomson's bellow set two streams of seamen pouring for'ard along the gangways and before the marines had finished clumping down from the poop the wash-deck pump had cleansed the stains from the gratings and they were back in place. Jeremiah, when he came to think about it afterwards, realised that the whole ceremony had occupied only five minutes. He had been disgusted to find himself excited by the spectacle of inflicted pain and confessed as much when the flogging was being discussed in the midshipmen's mess.

'Why, it was no bloodier than a cockfight!' said FitzJames, who was four years younger than Jeremiah. 'What's six? Wait till you've seen a man given fifty.'

'He won't see it in *Indefatigable*,' said Benedict.

'But of course there was no flogging at all in a smuggling brig,' said Charles Paddon with a palpable sneer.

'No—there was no need for it,' retorted Jeremiah.

'And there's for you, young Charles,' Delamere said. 'In the old *Sandwich*, seventy-four—bloody old bitch!—I've seen a poor devil given three hundred lashes. The buzz was that he died at the two-hundredth.'

Benedict pulled a face. 'The better for him.' He turned to Jeremiah. 'You must understand that six lashes is the minimum for Cattermole's offence. Captain Pellew couldn't give less—and there'll be plenty of hands on our lower-deck saying he was too soft with Cattermole. They all know he don't like flogging.'

'That's it, you know.' FitzJames's air of judicial sapience went oddly with his schoolboy countenance. 'Flog 'em too much and they mutiny, too little and they take advantage. There's flogging captains and there's soft 'uns.'

'There's only one Edward Pellew,' said

Benedict positively, 'and *Indefatigable* ain't like other ships.'

And that, Jeremiah found, was the monition that met him wherever his duties took him about the frigate: she wasn't like other ships, being in all respects a great deal better.

'You young gentlemen,' said Mr Hannay the boatswain, 'will find most wessels puts a stopper on the backstay with five turns, but on board this ship we puts six, which is right and proper.'

'Pull yer weight, yer lazy bugger!' growled a seaman to the next man hauling on the mainsheet. 'Yer in *Indefatigable* now!'

Captain Pellew, at the close of instruction in taking the noon sight (a daily ritual for all five midshipmen), hinted at a similar habit of thought.

'You're doing well,' said he, 'but not well enough for this ship. See to it. And mark this—I'll have all my midshipmen able to perform the duty of any other man on board—' He paused and the brown eyes twinkled. 'Belay that. I'll except the chaplain's.'

From the hints and tales that came to his ears during his first week at sea Jeremiah was soon persuaded that he was indeed fortunate in his ship. Delamere's stories of the midshipmen's mess on board *Sandwich*, in which he had served before joining the frigate, painted such a Bedlam of vice and uproar that *Indefatigable*'s after-cockpit seemed a veritable Arcadia by comparison; and this despite the sickening smell from the bilges and the fact that the red-painted table had served, and would serve again, as the surgeon's operating bench.

The senior midshipman set the tone of this mess, and though Delamere and the others accepted his rule with an amused tolerance it was a firm rule none the less. Benedict's professed admiration for the tenets laid down by Tom Paine in *The Rights of Man* (downright treason in a King's officer, declared Caldecott) sparked off many a heated if uninformed debate; and where—according to Delamere—the midshipmen of *Sandwich* would have spent their leisure in fighting over the rival attractions of the Portsmouth whore-houses Captain Pellew's young gentlemen argued about naval strategy, stag-hunting, George Selwyn's latest *amour*, the use of a cutlass in parrying a thrust in tierce, whether Parliament was really a nest of scoundrels as Horne Tooke had asserted, and a host of similarly varied topics.

'In my opinion,' Benedict explained to Jeremiah on one occasion, 'this is a sort of junior wardroom, and we talk and behave accordingly. We're all supposed to be gentlemen, after—'

He stopped abruptly and bit his lip.

Jeremiah grinned. 'I'll study to conform, Ben,' he said.

On all formal occasions the midshipmen were 'Mister' to each other, but in the after-cockpit, if there were no visitors present, the honorific was dropped and nicknames were in order. Inevitably Jeremiah became Jerry. Only one member of the mess persistently addressed him as 'Mister Coghlan,' and there was excuse for this in the fact that Charles Paddon was on *Indefatigable*'s books as officer's servant. Jeremiah was aware that influential parents or those closely acquainted with a post-captain could arrange for their sons to enter the Navy in this way pending their rating as midshipmen, so acquiring the necessary sea-time, and a purist might hold that a full midshipman was superior in the naval hierarchy; but he understood very well that young Paddon's 'mister' was a sarcasm. However warmly Benedict and the rest accepted him, Charles Paddon of Trenythan resented his intrusion among gentlemen born.

There was little to trouble Jeremiah in this, and indeed he had small leisure to think about it in the first four weeks of his service in *Indefatigable*.

For Edward Pellew's recipe for an orderly and efficient ship lay not so much in sparing the lash as in continuously exercising his crew. With the weather of that stormy November creating incessant need for altering or shortening sail there was little sail-drill ordered, but gun-drill occupied every moment of the watch-on-deck when they were not aloft or tailing-on to sheets and halyards. In this Midshipman Coghlan played his part, no idle one. Two of the big 24-pounders were his particular charges and, as the toiling gun-crews went through the motions of firing, reloading, and running-out, Pellew striding along the line of guns, would strike the shoulder of this man or that, falling him out as wounded or dead, and Jeremiah would jump to take his place. As layer or trainer, in ramming and sponging and hauling on the relieving-tackles, he became adept in this mock fighting. Mr Packe, the gunner, approved enthusiastically of this emphasis on gunnery, which (he said) was the prime winner of sea-fights, and his captain went even further.

'The grandson of this fellow,' he said once, stopping to pat the cascabel of one of Jeremiah's two guns, 'will be more important in naval warfare than seamanship itself. If ever you command a ship, Mr Coghlan, train your gun-crews until they can load and run-out in their sleep.'

Adverse winds and a succession of gales, forerunners of a stormy winter, hampered the frigate's passage to the rendezvous off Ushant with the blockading fleet. On a morning of scudding cloud and tall broken seas Jeremiah watched the frigate's cutter heading across to the Vice-Admiral's flagship with the clouds of spray flying from her plunging bows and the receding line of 74's stretching beyond into the grey haze. Pellew's brow was as dark as the lowering skies when he embarked; Sir John's ten ships had been found far to leeward of the rendezvous, a good twenty leagues offshore and impotent to attack if the French decided to come out. When he returned on board the captain's brow was blacker still, and his curt orders to make sail and bear away rasped like a file.

Next morning, with half-a-gale blowing, they sighted *Amazon* off Pointe St Mathieu and her captain, Reynolds, came on board to report. Half-an-hour later *Amazon* was racing southward, back to her watch over L'Orient eighty sea-miles away, and *Indefatigable* was running before the wind towards the French coast.

'We'll be under fire in an hour,' Benedict told Jeremiah and Caldecott as the three snatched a hurried breakfast in the after-cockpit. 'Captain Pellew won't rest until he's seen for himself what's going on in Brest. *Amazon* spotted something. Right up the Goulette we go until we can look into the Rade.'

'How d'you know?' Jeremiah asked curiously.

Caldecott raised his eyebrows. 'I thought it was known to you, Jerry,' he said, 'that Ben lurks with his ear to the bulkhead of the captain's privy. Since this abuts on the day-cabin and acts as a sounding-board, he's able to overhear—'

'Pipe down, Cal,' Benedict interrupted without rancour. 'Any fool could tell that Pellew would run up the Goulette as soon as we were back on station. It'll be the tenth time. And you'll comprehend, Jerry,' he added, 'that in a ship that's a wooden box a hundred and fifty feet by forty, crammed with nigh on three hundred men, what's talked of in the wardroom don't take long to reach the gunroom—and the lower deck too.'

'There goes eight bells,' said Caldecott as the four double clangs sounded from the deck above. 'Drink up, gentlemen, if you please.'

They gulped the last of the muddy cocoa and hurried on deck to relieve Delamere, FitzJames and Paddon, who had had the morning watch.

Benedict's forecast proved totally correct. Within minutes of Jeremiah's arrival on deck the low grey line of the Brittany coast showed above the tossing seas on the larboard bow.

'We're well into Camaret Bay,' said Benedict. 'The Toulinguet point's somewhere to starboard.'

Jermiah's smuggling cruises had taken him no farther west than Roscoff on the north Finisterre coast, and he listened with interest to the senior midshipman's explanation of the Brest harbourage. The inner bay or Rade, where the French ships were lying, was six miles long and only accessible from the outer bay of Camaret by the rocky passage of La Goulette, less than a mile wide. Ships coming out of Brest into Camaret Bay, and knowing (as the French knew) that an enemy fleet was awaiting them to westward, would probably try to get to sea through the Passage d'Iroise by which *Indefatigable* had come in or by the narrower Raz de Sein to southward.

'But they can't do either while these westerlies keep blowing,' Benedict said. 'If the wind should change—'

A yell from the first lieutenant, followed by the shrilling of the bosuns' pipes and the stirring *rafale* of the drums beating to quarters, ended his exposition. Jeremiah ran to his battle station behind the 24-pounders aft on the larboard side, dodging through the orderly rush of seamen. The guns were loaded but not run out. Ahead, a scant three miles away, the land seemed to rise in a continuous blue line and the frigate was speeding straight towards it. Then the dark notch of a gap appeared and swiftly widened, a channel flanked by low cliffs with squat grey buildings topping them on either hand. As Jeremiah's eye picked out the forts he saw an orange flash from one of them, bright in the dull morning light, and heard the heavy thump of the gun.

'Knows us by now, the buggers,' chuckled

Camden, the stumpy baldheaded bosun's mate who was standing just behind Jeremiah. 'They keeps one up the spout, I reckon, against we pays a call.'

The second fort fired as he spoke. Jeremiah could see nothing of the fall of shot; *Indefatigable*'s onward rush had carried her almost to the mile-wide entrance of the Goulette before the guns spoke again, and even then there was no sign of the 32-pounder balls. He reflected that to hit a target moving as fast as the frigate with a missile the size of a plum-pudding, at half-a-mile's distance, could be no easy task, and the thought quelled the mixture of excitement and apprehension that was his reaction to this baptism of fire.

The craggy shores of the narrows slipped past on either beam and the slow banging of the guns ceased as the forts were left astern. Pellew swung himself into the foremast shrouds and climbed to the masthead. Suddenly the cliffs to starboard fell back and they were out in the wider waters of the Rade, with the houses and alleys of a considerable town climbing a low hill on the larboard shore three or four miles away. From the grey waters at the foot of the town rose a dark forest of masts growing from a long mass of giant hulls. From Jeremiah's low station it was impossible to distinguish separate vessels, but he knew he was looking at the French fleet, Admiral Morard de Galles' fighting-ships that would sail for the invasion of England if ever they got the chance.

'Very well, Mr Thomson!'

Pellew's shout from the masthead set the first lieutenant bellowing orders. *Indefatigable* heeled sharply as the helm was put over, swung her bows towards the mouth of the Goulette, and thrust to windward on the larboard tack. Pellew dodged a shower of spray as he stepped down from the shrouds and crossed the quarterdeck to Thomson.

'Fourteen of the line and ten frigates at least,' Jeremiah heard him say. 'I wish to God I knew what they're up to.'

The passage back through the Goulette, tacking incessantly against a strong foul wind, was a revelation to the late deckhand of a brig of what superb seamanship and a perfectly trained crew could do. The gauntlet-run past the forts came almost as a relief after that daring scrape through the narrows. But this time the reduced speed gave the French gunners a better chance. A crescendo yowling close overhead made Jeremiah duck involuntarily (to the delight of the men at the guns and his own confusion) and a musical twang told of a parted stay. It was their only casualty, and by noon the frigate had brought Pointe St Mathieu on her starboard quarter and was out in the open sea with the gale still freshening from the west.

The bad weather persisted day after day

while November passed into December. With occasional sulky lulls, rough seas and westerly gales pursued *Indefatigable* as she patrolled the dangerous lee shore from St Mathieu to the Penmarcks south of Audierne Bay, where at intervals of three days she made rendezvous with *Amazon* and received her report. A small armed lugger, the *Duke of York*, bore such reports to Colpoys and his squadron far distant beyond the western horizon.

On one occasion Pellew sent *Amazon* to watch Brest while he sailed on southward to make contact with *Revolutionnaire* and *Phoebe* off L'Orient and Rochefort. Twice in this period he ran the passage of the Goulette, losing his foretopmast the second time; and the result of his observation of the Brest shipping was that *Amazon* and *Revolutionnaire* were summoned to join him off Brest. What Caldecott called 'Benedict's privy-telegraph' conveyed the reason for this to the midshipmen's mess.

'Five line-of-battles and three frigates have got into Brest,' Benedict told them. 'That'll be Richery's squadron from the Ile d'Aix. We'll have action soon, if Colpoys is game—which I doubt.'

There was action, though not of the sort anticipated by the after-cockpit, on the day following this pronouncement. Captain Cole of the *Revolutionnaire* had come on board, the two frigates being hove-to four leagues off Camaret.

At two bells of the first watch Jeremiah Coghlan and Charles Paddon were summoned to the captain's cabin, where they found Pellew frowning over a chart with the grizzled captain of *Revolutionnaire* and Bolton, *Indefatigable*'s third lieutenant. Bolton was only a year older than Jeremiah, bullet-headed and fresh-coloured.

'I'm told you speak French, Mr Paddon,' Pellew said without preamble. 'Fluently?'

'I believe so, sir,' Paddon drawled. 'My tutor was the Marquis de Plombiers, a Royalist refugee.'

'Hum. And you, Mr Coghlan?'

'I'm a poor hand at the French tongue, sir,' said Jeremiah. 'I speak Breton, though.'

'Ah. Read that to us aloud.'

Pellew folded a crumpled sheet so that part of the writing on it was displayed, and passed it to the midshipman. Jeremiah read out the five words written in large capitals.

'"*Ni zo Bretoned, tud kaled.*"'

'The meaning, please?'

Jeremiah considered quickly. 'We are the Bretons, sir, a hardy race.'

Pellew grinned. 'The "sir" being your own interpolation. So that's the password, Cole. Does it mean this fellow's a Breton?'

'Hard to say.' Cole rubbed his chin. 'The rest of the message is in ordinary French.'

'With respect, sir,' Bolton ventured

nervously, 'since I don't speak a word of either lingo, and both might be needed—'

'Just so, Mr Bolton. Better take 'em both.' Pellew's sharp glance went from one to the other of the midshipmen. 'You'll go with the boat party tonight. See that you're ready. A man's to be taken off from the French shore—but Mr Bolton will give you your orders. Carry on.'

3

''Vast pulling,' said Bolton hoarsely, and the six oarsmen rested their oars.

The lieutenant stood up, balancing to the heave of the boat as the black waves swept under her and on shoreward, cupping his eyes with his hands the better to scan the uneven outline of the rocky coast a scant cable-length ahead.

'Rock pillar big as a church—sandy cove either side—western cove's the one,' he muttered; he had repeated the words more than once since the boat had left *Indefatigable*'s side half-an-hour ago.

'Looks a likely place on the stabb'd bow, sir,' said Camden from the bows.

'Keep your voice down, damn you!' Bolton hissed sharply. 'Give way, all.'

He sat down, easing the tiller a trifle to

larboard as the men recommenced pulling. The midshipmen squeezed on the stern thwart on either side of him sat taut and silent, peering into the darkness whence came the dull thunder of a moderate surf breaking on a beach. It was a luminous darkness, for a moon just past her full shed a faint radiance through the low clouds that hurried overhead. The onshore wind, though strong, would not make a landing difficult and the sea was slight compared with yesterday's scurrying breakers. Considering the weather of the past weeks, thought Jeremiah, there could hardly have been a better night for the venture.

Bolton had explained to his junior officers the circumstances of this mission. Two days ago *Revolutionnaire* had been approached by a Breton fishing-smack out of Crozon and a letter delivered to her captain. Its writer, unnamed, claimed to be a Breton Royalist with secret information concerning the French fleet in Brest, which he would deliver to the English commander in return for a passage to England. A boat should be sent to take him from a cove on the coast two miles north of the fishing village of Le Conquet, which village was two miles north of Pointe St Mathieu and fifteen miles west of Brest; and the cove was the westerly one of two which were separated by an unmistakable column of rock shaped like a church. The writer would be there every night from midnight until two in the morning to await the boat, which would identify herself with the words *Ni zo Bretoned*, bringing the counter-identification of *Tud kaled* from the writer.

To Jeremiah's mind it was unlikely that a Chouan had been able to obtain information of any value about the intentions of Admiral De Galles; doubtless Captain Pellew's intense desire for some hint, however slight, of such intentions had led him to risk his third officer, nine men, and the frigate's smallest boat on the chance of getting it.

'That's it,' Bolton said in an undertone. 'The church pillar.'

Jeremiah could feel his body tense, trembling a little. Bolton was nervous, over-anxious, or he would have realised that voices could hardly carry above the increasing roar of the surf. The black outline of low cliffs showed near at hand against the sky, at their foot a pair of pale oval blotches with a jagged pinnacle of rock, discernibly spire-like, rising between them.

'We'll beach her,' said Bolton, one hand feeling for his sword-hilt. 'A cutlass apiece, Camden, soon as we're ashore. Hunt and Nixon will stay by the boat. The rest will come with me.'

Jeremiah reflected that in Bolton's place he would have ordered the boat to lie offshore when it had landed him. He could see the lofty tip of the pinnacle against the sky's faint pallor now, and feel the stronger surge of the waves as they neared the beach. The glimmer of sand east of the tall pinnacle passed from sight behind its jagged foot-rocks, Bolton brought the boat stern-on to a following wave, and amid a flurry of surf her forefoot ploughed into the sandy beach. Camden was ashore and hanging onto her bow, the seamen were overside and running her up with the next wave helping them. Bolton scrambled for'ard across the thwarts with Jeremiah and Paddon behind him and they sprang down into soft sand with seawater bubbling round their ankles.

There was a faint clinking of metal and Jeremiah found a cutlass hilt in his hand. He wondered as he gripped it what use it could be. Pellew had been right to allow no firearms but neither steel nor firearms were likely to help nine British sailors discovered on enemy territory five leagues from a big French naval base.

'Come on, then,' said Bolton, beginning to lead his little party up the beach.

It was much darker here under the loom of the cliffs than it had been out on the water, and even against the paler darkness of the cove's sandy floor the moving figures of the seamen were only indeterminate patches of shadow. The sand, gently sloping, seemed to run up for a hundred yards or more into a terminal chaos of huge fallen rocks at the foot of the cliffs, rocks as big as cottages; a break in the ragged black line of the cliff-top, just discernible against the sky, suggested to Jeremiah a path descending to the cove and its possible convenience to smugglers. On their left as they walked was a low neck of rock connecting the pinnacle with the main cliff and so separating the two coves, and some obscure instinct made the lieutenant, with the two midshipmen behind him and the seamen at their heels, keep close to this neck.

They were halfway up the beach when Bolton halted so suddenly that his followers cannoned into each other.

'*Still!*' he hissed urgently, and they all stood motionless, listening.

'Thought I heard a sound,' Bolton said; and then, irritably, 'Why don't this fellow come out and show himself?'

'Maybe he's waiting for our word, sir,' Paddon suggested.

'Maybe. Yes. Mr Coghlan, speak out that password.'

Jeremiah spoke loudly enough for his voice to carry fifty yards and top the rumble of the surf. '*Ni zo Bretoned!*'

The weird echo from the cliff-face mingled with the sound of scuffling in the darkness below it. A man burst suddenly out from among the big rocks, running with the speed of desperation and yelling at the top of his voice as he came.

'Gare! Gare! Embûche! Emb—'

A stab of flame from behind him and the bang of a musket cut short his utterance. He leapt and dropped like a sack ten paces from the landing-party. Instantly a multiple explosion of musket-fire echoed and blazed from the foot of the crags. Bolton sank down with a groan, a seaman reeled past Jeremiah to plunge face-downwards on the sand. In the blackness ahead movement stirred and men came scrambling through the boulder-chaos, a dozen, perhaps more.

'On, men—at 'em, into 'em!' Paddon screeched, waving his cutlass.

Jeremiah collared him as he dashed forward, felt his fist strike bone in the brief scuffle, swung the boy to the rightabout and urged him seaward with a shove in the back.

'To the boat!' he roared; and, louder still, 'Boat ahoy! Push her off and stand by!' The French were slow coming on, blinded by musket-flashes, uncertain how many they had to deal with. 'Camden, Leary, take Mr Bolton. And Camden—take the boat well out, then pull back into the other cove, east of this pinnacle. Lively, now.'

'Aye, sir,' Camden said. 'But you—'

'I'll be there,' said Jeremiah. 'Move, man, move!'

Bent double, he dashed away, scuttling like a giant crab across the ten yards of sand to the neck between the coves. His fingers groped across rock, found a tall shallow niche. He crammed himself into it as best he could and froze, motionless, with his chin on his chest and his hat-brim shading his face.

His actions in that crowded ten seconds had been dictated by one consideration: Pellew wanted that spy, that Breton. The man lying motionless twenty paces from him might still be alive and able to deliver his information. If Jeremiah's divergence from the retreat had not been observed, if the French did not stop to examine the fallen man—

And here came the French with a shout, running and stumbling down towards the boat. They hadn't paused for the lengthy business of reloading muskets and the little crowd of rushing figures passed the Breton without check. As the last of them sped yelling past his hiding-place Jeremiah straightened himself and stepped forward. Instantly he halted, rigid. A man had walked out from the boulders and was approaching the figure sprawled in the sand. A sergeant or an officer, probably. He stopped by the prostrate man. Down the beach on Jeremiah's right the shouting had intensified and the officer started to run. The sudden movement on his flank alerted him, but he had no time to dodge the descending sweep of the cutlass that cut into him between neck and shoulder.

Afterwards the reactions of his first killing were to assail Jeremiah—the shuddering sickness as he recalled the crunch of steel into flesh and bone, the choking, bubbling cry. At the time his mind was occupied with the urgency of action. He flung away the cutlass and hoisted the Breton on his shoulder; a slight, skinny man, limp and no great burden. The low rocks of the neck were slippery with pockets of wet seaweed but he was up and stumbling among the rocks on the farther side when the bang of a musket sounded, muted by the intervening mass of the pinnacle on his left. That meant, surely, that the boat was clear of the shore. His feet sank into sand, in front was the white glimmer of the surf. He floundered down the beach as hard as he could go, heading away to the right to put distance between himself and the neck of rock in case of pursuit. On the water's edge he set down his burden and tore open the front of his pea-jacket so that his shirt would make some sort of mark for Camden and the boat—if they came.

The few minutes he had to wait seemed an hour. The boat took shape, heaving towards him on the waves, and with the Breton in his arms he waded in waist-deep. Shouts echoed above the noise of the surf as he and his prize were dragged aboard in a welter of seawater, the flash and crack of a musket followed. But now the oars had tugged her clear of the breakers and her bow was pointing seaward for the long pull back to the waiting frigate.

Jeremiah took over the tiller from a silent figure in the stern-sheets. 'Mr Bolton?' he asked.

'He'll do, sir,' said Camden. 'Bullet grazed his scalp. We had to leave Higgins, sir.'

'Higgins was a deader anyway,' said a voice. 'Shot through the eye.'

'You brought off the Frog neat enough, sir,' Camden said. 'D'ye reckon he's alive?'

'I don't know. Nothing we can do about him till we're back on board, and the sooner we're there the better. Put your backs into it.'

It was the better part of an hour before the denser blackness of the frigate's hull loomed out of the dark. In that time Charles Paddon, hunched on the stern thwart beside Jeremiah, had not spoken a word.

4

The Breton spy died twenty minutes after being brought on board *Indefatigable*, of internal haemorrhage according to Tierney, the frigate's surgeon. This interval, during which Pellew was with the surgeon and his patient, gave Jeremiah time to change into dry clothes before he was summoned to the captain's cabin.

'I understand Mr Bolton was incapacitated early in this affair,' Pellew said. 'As next in seniority, Mr Coghlan, I'll have a report from you, if you please.'

Jeremiah, cudgelling unaccustomed brains, told the story as concisely as he could. The captain listened without interruption. Then he looked up, frowning.

'When I ask for a report, Mr Coghlan, I expect no omissions. Mr Paddon has already complained—to the first lieutenant, as was correct—that in the course of this skirmish you struck him. Why have you not mentioned this?'

Jeremiah moistened his lips. Damn Paddon. Couldn't the fool have kept quiet?

'When the shots were fired, sir,' he said, trying to choose the right words, 'Mr Paddon wanted to attack. He called the men to advance and started forward. I caught hold of him and pulled him back. If I hit him it was by accident—it was very dark, sir, and there wasn't time for ceremony.'

'I see.' Pellew rubbed his chin. 'Well, I have to take notice of such complaints. Bear in mind, Mr Coghlan, that one officer doesn't strike another when on duty. And off duty—since, as I take it, Mr Paddon considers himself affronted—there will be no pursuance of this matter. Do you understand me?'

'Yes, sir.'

'Good. That being so, it gives me pleasure to commend the rest of your behaviour in this matter.'

Jeremiah reddened with pleasure. 'Thank you, sir.'

Pellew nodded. 'Carry on, Mr Coghlan.'

But Jeremiah lingered, nerving himself. 'Sir—'

The captain looked up. 'Well?'

'Sir, was it any use? Did the Breton—' His voice faltered before Pellew's stare.

The captain hesitated a moment, then threw himself back in his chair. 'It's but just that you should have an answer,' he said. 'Yes, he spoke before he died, one sentence. "Fifteen thousand troops ready to embark."'

'Then they'll come out—I beg your pardon, sir.'

'The probability is they'll sail within the week. It could be for a landing in England, or possibly Ireland. God knows if the Admiral—' Pellew checked himself. 'Mr Tierney tells me the Breton had been tortured—thumb-screws, of all things. So you see they'd forced him to act as a decoy. At the last he had the guts to warn you. He was a brave man.'

When he returned to the after-cockpit Jeremiah found Benedict and Paddon there. He had already decided what course to take with Paddon, and he took it at once.

'Mr Paddon, I believe I chanced to strike you

by accident on the beach yonder. I'm sorry for it.'

Paddon regarded him stonily. A purple-red graze on his cheekbone stood out angrily on his pallor.

'You need to be, by God!' he said unpleasantly. 'I'm not in the habit of being assaulted by—'

'Apology offered and accepted,' Benedict cut in loudly. 'In my opinion, Charles,' he added judicially, 'you'd do well to thank Jerry for saving your life.'

Paddon swung on his heel without a word and began to prepare himself for turning-in.

Considering the thing later, Jeremiah perceived that the accidental blow was only a fraction of his offence in Paddon's eyes. The tale of the shore expedition was all over the ship within minutes of its return. Jeremiah's stock was high and Paddon's low. At the decisive moment he had been right and Paddon wrong. The fisherman's son had succeeded and the gentleman had failed. This was what Charles Paddon could not forgive.

CHAPTER THREE

FIREWORK NIGHT

1

'There is now in Brest 21 sail of the line appearing ready for sea, 2 of them three-deckers, and 2 other three-deckers with yards and topmasts down . . . We were so near in as to be fired at from both sides of the Goulette and could most distinctly see everything in the port. The ships all appear clean painted . . . It is much to be regretted that this fleet could not be intercepted.'

So wrote Captain Sir Edward Pellew in his report to Admiralty, carried home by the frigate *Amazon* on December 12th. A junior captain could venture no plainer hint that his Admiral, Lord Bridport, should be stirred from his winter lethargy and the Channel Fleet sent to sea. Whether the great expedition now preparing in Brest was intended for the subjugation of Britain's one remaining ally Portugal, or for the Channel, or for a landing in Ireland to unite with the Catholic rebels there, no one could tell; but in any case Colpoys's ten of the line could do nothing against an armada like this, though he would be expected to try.

His ships had been battered week after week by the worst succession of autumn and winter gales in living memory, and Sir John himself was not the commander to lead his squadron in an attack both desperate and doomed.

Captain Pellew frowningly considered these things as he took his accustomed exercise on *Indefatigable*'s quarterdeck. A three-day gale had blown itself out yesterday afternoon and on this morning of December 16th the salt air had fallen strangely still. Through the slowly-lightening darkness the frigate, wearing topsails and outer jib, swooped uncomfortably over the smooth black waves that rolled into Camaret bay with just enough of the fitful breeze to give her steerage way. There was nothing *Indefatigable* could do against the French either, reflected Pellew. He had only *Revolutionnaire* with him now, and she was stationed outside the bay ready to take the news, when it came, to Colpoys's squadron forty miles offshore, after which frigates and ships-of-the-line were to unite at the appointed rendezvous off Ushant. The dispositions were made and he could only go on waiting and watching. He turned his thoughts to his ship and her crew, and after a moment summoned the first lieutenant from the little group of dark figures over on the lee side of the quarterdeck.

'Good morning, sir,' said Thomson, falling into step beside his pacing senior. The captain had come on deck fifteen minutes ago, but his officers knew better than to trespass on his attention or the deck sacred to his morning walk.

'Morning, Mr Thomson,' said Pellew. 'Anything to report?'

'Course east by north, sir, but it's not easy to hold it in these light airs. Masthead reported Pointe St Matthew fine on the larboard bow just before you came on deck. I've a man at the topgallant crosstrees, sir.'

'Um. Ship's company happy?'

'Happy but spoiling for lack of fighting,' Thomson hesitated. 'There's this business in the gunroom, sir—Mr Paddon and Mr Coghlan. *They're* spoiling for a fight, I reckon.'

'What—there's been no challenge?' Pellew questioned sharply.

'Not that I know of, sir. It's just that they won't work together as they should. Stiff and bristling, like dogs. I reckon it's Mr Paddon that's to blame. The men see it and it unsettles them. To my mind—'

'Damn and blast them!' snapped Pellew. 'They'll be made to work together or I'll know the reason why, Mr Thomson!'

'Aye, sir,' Thomson said dubiously. 'I've had 'em up and dressed 'em down a dozen times and it does no good. Mr Paddon—'

'Young Paddon's as high and mighty as his father was. You served with Sir John, I fancy.'

'I was third under him in the old *Tamar*, sir. A—a fine gentleman.'

'Too damned fine by—' Pellew checked himself. 'Dead these sixteen years and *de mortuis* and so on, but he was mad about blood.'

'Blood, sir?' Thomson was puzzled.

'Call it family if you like. Paddon had the blood of kings in his veins, or so he claimed. Direct descendant of one Richard, King of Rome, who was king of Cornwall in the Year One. King George himself—God bless him—was a johnny-come-lately by John Paddon's measure. Damned fool!' added Pellew, whose ancestors had been merchants in Flushing.

Thomson pondered. 'If young Paddon thinks like his dad, then he reckons he's a deal too fine to be junior to a fisherman's lad like Coghlan. Is that it, sir?'

'More than likely,' said Pellew, and fingered his chin. 'I wonder if I were to—'

The rustle and flap of the mizzen topsail overhead, followed instantly by the first lieutenant's roar at the helmsman to keep her full-and-bye, left his problem unstated.

'I'm going up to the foretop,' he said abruptly.

The darkness was fast receding before the advance of a winter dawn, though it was not yet light enough to make out the features of the men who squatted or leaned along the for'ard rail, the watch-on-deck. Pellew swung himself into the foremast shrouds, climbing with an agility that belied his forty years. When his head came level with the wooden platform of the foretop he was aware that it was already occupied.

'Who's that?' he demanded.

'Coghlan, sir.' The harsh voice was curiously like his own.

'Shove over, then,' grunted Pellew, hauling himself into the top. 'What are you doing here?'

'It's my watch below, sir. Mr Thomson said I might come up.'

'Anything to report?'

Pellew spoke with casual irony. Already he was peering ahead, where between dark cloud and dark sea a line of blacker darkness indicated the eastern coasts of Camaret Bay.

'Yes, sir,' said Jeremiah. 'The wind's changed.'

The captain turned sharply. 'Don't play the fool with me, Mr Coghlan!' he snapped. 'The wind's where it was, as you very well know.'

'It's changed over the land,' Jeremiah said positively. 'Easterly, it's blowing. It'll meet us any time now, sir.'

'What makes you so sure?' inquired Pellew, with less austerity; he had learned to respect the weather-wisdom of Cornish fisherfolk.

'I can smell it.' As Jeremiah spoke a more substantial smell of coffee, borne on some inconsequent updraught, rose transiently to the foretop and reminded him that he was cold and hungry. 'Er— with your leave, sir—'

'Down you go,' said Pellew with a grin.

Jeremiah's lanky form vanished down the shrouds.

Pellew turned again to his scrutiny of the lightening horizon, reflecting as he did so that he had missed a chance of administering a fatherly reproof instead of an official reprimand to one of two damned young idiots. The matter passed from his mind at once, one of the thousand petty worries of a man who ruled the destinies of three hundred of his fellow men. If young Coghlan was right, the first touch of the easterly might even now be ruffling the waters of the Rade. If the French were as ready to come out as he thought, the signal to up-anchor and make sail might be at their admiral's masthead this moment. It was bitter cold up there in the half darkness, but he stayed while the overcast sky paled and the nearing coast took shape—that so familiar coast, with the narrow breach of the Goulette now discernible. Eight bells of the morning watch clanged from the deck below, and hardly a minute later the lookout's hail came from the crosstrees overhead. Pellew had seen the fleck of white that appeared in the notch of the Goulette, and his glass showed him the ruffle of wind-blown sea between him and the French ship.

'Mr Thomson!' he roared. 'Starboard two points—and stand by to make sail!'

The forerunners of the easterly wind made the frigate heel as she turned on her new course. Pellew steadied his glass. Astern of that first sail came another. And a third. Now a taller vessel—three frigates and a third-rate were out in the bay. It might mean only that De Galles was making a gesture, giving vent to his exasperation at the impertinent vessel that spied so persistently on his operations. Or it might mean—

But in any case it was not *Indefatigable*'s business to come to close quarters with odds like these. Pellew raced down the shrouds, bellowing orders as he went. The first topmen were springing up past him as he dropped to the deck. Main courses, topgallants, royals, and spanker spread and filled with that rising east wind and the frigate, foaming round in a half-circle sped back the way she had come. Pellew, on the quarterdeck, kept his glass on the white specks astern until they merged with the grey-and-white of the sea horizon.

'Five frigates and the third-rate,' Jeremiah heard him say to the first lieutenant. 'No more have come out.'

The news that the French were coming out at last had brought all six midshipmen onto the quarterdeck, where they were clustered with ears and eyes alert.

'A feint, sir,' suggested Thomson. 'Or maybe just an exercise.'

'But tide's making now,' Jeremiah muttered into the ear of Paddon, who stood next to him. 'They'll not bring the big 'uns out through the Goulette until the ebb, which is this afternoon.'

Paddon raised one delicate eyebrow. 'Indeed, Mr Coghlan?' he said coldly. 'No doubt you know best, as always.'

The captain's voice prevented any further interchange.

'If I were Admiral de Galles,' said Pellew, 'I'd not bring my three-deckers through the Goulette while the tide's making, Mr Thomson. This afternoon's his time, depend upon it.'

Mr Coghlan was careful not to look at Mr Paddon.

2

Dusk of a stormy winter day was already falling when *Indefatigable* came creeping in round the white-rimmed shoals off Pointe St Mathieu and thrust her prying bows once more into Camaret Bay. The east wind was blowing strong and gusty, knocking up a confused and choppy sea as it met the rollers that still marked the impetus of bygone westerly gales. The frigate shouldered close-hauled through the uneasy waves at no more than three or four knots under her reefed topsails and jibs, making short boards and keeping as close to the northern shore as her captain's intimate knowledge of the shoals allowed. She was cleared for action, guns loaded but not run out.

Revolutionnaire had been despatched with her urgent message to Colpoys and his squadron and *Indefatigable* was alone. Her part in the present emergency was over. A frigate's duty was to locate and report the position of an enemy fleet and leave the ships of the line to fight it out; but Edward Pellew was not satisfied that his duty had been done until his utmost endeavour had been made. He was up in the swaying foretop now, chilled through and through by the biting wind, peering for the first sight of Morard de Galles's great fleet.

To Pellew's mind it was a practical certainty that the French admiral was bent on putting to sea immediately; to count on this rare easterly wind enduring for a further twenty-four hours would be the act of a fool, and De Galles was no fool. But he had to make sure, and that was one reason why he had brought *Indefatigable* slinking through the twilight back into the bay instead of patrolling outside. The other reason was more subtle. Here was a score and more of great ships that had lain blockaded in port for month after month, their crews mainly inexperienced, the officers uncertain of their men. On board they carried 15,000 soldiers and—probably—vast quantities of stores for whatever enterprise they were bound upon. Some confusion was certain to accompany the setting-forth of such a fleet, and in that confusion it might just be possible for a well-handled frigate to strike a blow at the enemy.

'Sa-a-il ho! Broad o' the stabb'd beam!' yelled the lookout above him.

Far to southward a broken line of white lay on the horizon, glimmering through the fast-falling darkness. Pellew's numbed hands could hardly steady the glass on it, and remembering that the masthead lookout must be even colder than his captain he ordered the man to go down.

'Couple o' dozen sail yonder, sir,' said the lookout through chattering teeth, as he descended past the foretop.

Pellew stayed aloft for five minutes more. In the thickening murk it was impossible to make out more of that mass of shipping ten miles away. What was De Galles up to, with his fleet so far to the south? The Iroise passage by which *Indefatigable* had entered the bay was wide and safe, the usual exit from Camaret Bay; yet the French ships must have turned away from it as they emerged from the Goulette, turned southward towards the tricky and narrow Raz de Sein passage. De Galles, then, suspected that a strong enemy force awaited him outside the

Iroise. That much the bold assurance of Pellew and his frigates had achieved. And if a fleet of big ships, two of them three-deckers, tried the Raz de Sein in darkness with a beam wind there was no knowing what might happen.

Pellew ran his eye along the dark coastline two miles on his larboard hand and identified the break of the Goulette. No vessel near that. The gleam of new white canvas that had revealed the Frenchmen to him would hardly have made him visible to them, for his much-patched topsails were stained dark by months of hard weather. He would cross the Goulette entrance and approach as if he was a laggard Frenchman out of Brest. What happened next must depend on chance.

Down on the after-deck at the break of the poop three young gentlemen were discussing their captain's intentions. Though they could see no sail from deck level the lookout's hail had been enough to assure them that the French fleet was indeed out of Brest and in Camaret Bay.

'We're cleared for action, dear boy,' said Caldecott, stamping his feet to warm them. 'Red Ned wouldn't do that unless he means to have a crack at them.'

'Well, if he does get in among 'em,' said Jeremiah sceptically, 'what can he do?'

FitzJames's head popped tortoise-like from the turned-up collar of his pea-jacket.

'Know what I'd do if I was Ned?' he squeaked. 'Up French colours, scoot in through the Goulette, and set fire to Brest. The old *Indy* can't well tackle a fleet of Frog seventy-fours but she could—'

'Thank you, Mr FitzJames.' A tall dark figure had paused for a moment in passing. 'I'll bear your strategy in mind. For the present, please to consider your own duty rather than mine.'

Pellew swung himself up the ladder to the quarterdeck where his four lieutenants were staring eagerly into the obscurity to leeward.

'Mr Thomson, I'll have her on the larboard tack, if you please. Course south by east. And Mr Thomson,' he added as the first lieutenant turned to bellow the orders, 'keep your voice down. From now on there will be no loud talking or shouting. Pass the word for'ard.'

At Thomson's hoarse commands the hands ran to the braces and the wheel brought *Indefatigable* smoothly round through stays until her reefed sails filled close-hauled on the new course. There was still light enough to make out the gullies in the low cliffs of the Pointe du Toulinguet when she brought it on the larboard bow, though she was three miles out to clear the dangerous Toulinguet shoal; and when Pellew had twice tacked again, placing her so that she had the dark southern flank of the headland for background as she approached the French ships, the nearest of the latter were hull-up from the deck. Pellew climbed to the foretop again. The sight before him from this higher elevation made him wrinkle his brow in puzzlement.

Across several square miles of black tossing sea were scattered at least three dozen big ships under varying degrees of sail, some in groups, some isolated, some in untidy lines. It was impossible to divine what manoeuvre they were about. Beyond them, as he knew, the southern coast of the bay reached out westward to end in the Pointe du Raz with its broken continuation of rocky islets and shoals. The sole exit here was by the narrow Raz de Sein, and there could be no doubt that the French admiral had decided to muster his fleet here in order to take them out through the Raz. That would necessitate getting them into line—several lines, since the passage was so tricky and there were so many of them. Presumably this was what he was now attempting; with little success, judging by the evident confusion. That was to be expected with the ill-trained crews, and the fast-fading light that by now made signal hoists all but unreadable would add to the confusion.

He made the best count he could and numbered seventeen line-of-battle ships, seven large vessels that were probably transports crammed with troops, thirteen frigates, and half-a-dozen smaller vessels, corvettes and the like. A fleet of forty and more. If only Bridport and Colpoys had been waiting off Ushant ready to swoop on them! Knowing both his seniors, he reflected that Admiral Lord Bridport would hardly sail with the Channel Fleet before Christmas, and that Sir John Colpoys would consider his duty done if he hung on the enemy flanks in the hope of snapping-up a straggler. Was there any effective action a single frigate could take?

Pellew tried to put himself in De Galles' place. It must be evident to De Galles that to attempt a night passage of the Raz with this disorderly rabble of great ships was to take an inordinate risk; a 74 or one of the two three-deckers aground in the channel could block the Raz and endanger the ships astern. The long delay in ordering his fleet had rendered the southern passage not merely inadvisable but impossible, and De Galles must either anchor and wait a full tide for his chance, or reverse his decision and head north to come out by the Iroise passage. And in the second case how could he inform this scattered and benighted fleet of his intention?

That question was answered almost instantly. Ahead, from somewhere beyond the nearer French ships, a rocket soared aloft, its bright column drifting sideways before the wind and its transient glare emphasising the darkness. Pellew chuckled and launched himself down the futtock-shrouds. He was issuing his first orders as he bounded up to the quarterdeck.

'Pass the word for the gunner. Mr Thomson, turn up all hands, if you please—no piping, use messengers. Mr Gaze, hoist the French colours. Mr Coghlan, there! Find Mr Paddon and send him aft.' The burly shape of Packe the gunner bobbed up at his elbow. 'Mr Packe, I want our firework stores brought aft here—all of them, rockets, port-fires, blue-lights. And slow-match and a tub of water.'

'Aye aye, sir.'

Jeremiah, trotting across the deck towards the hatchway in the dim light, encountered the first rush of the watch-below arriving on deck. A collision with some unidentified zealot sent him reeling against a lighter body which his weight sent flying to the deck. Jeremiah bent to assist this accidental victim to his feet and was thrust away with unexpected violence.

'God damn you for a clumsy lout!' snarled Charles Paddon, and ran on.

'You're to report to Captain Pellew, Mr Paddon!' Jeremiah shouted after him.

Paddon evidently heard him, for he made for the quarter-deck ladder without reply. The first lieutenant heard him too, and his singular throaty growl (replacing the usual bull-bellow) promised a dozen lashes to the next man to raise his voice above a whisper. Smarting under a double sense of injury, Jeremiah took up his station abaft the mainmast, handy to the two upper-deck guns which were his charge. The hands had gone to quarters quietly enough and Thomson's threat had effectively subdued any inclination to chatter, so he could clearly hear Pellew speaking on the quarterdeck a few feet above him.

'Prepare two rockets and two blue-lights, Mr Packe, and stand by. Now, Mr Paddon. I want that French lingo of yours loaded and ready to fire at the word. You'll stand here by me and if we're hailed by a Frenchman you'll reply in due form. Understand?'

'Yes, sir.'

'We'd better have name and port of departure ready. Anything to suggest?'

'Perhaps *Masquerade* would fit the occasion, sir. Out of—'

'Out of Brest with the Admiral's wig-powder, which he'd left behind.' Pellew chuckled softly. 'Not bad, young Charles. Make it so. *Sapiens qui prospicit*, eh?—Mr Talley,' he added to the quartermaster standing beside the helm, 'bring her half-a-point to starboard. I want her taken between the nearer vessel, on the larboard bow, and the fellow farther off to leeward.'

The first lieutenant's hoarse voice spoke. 'If we're closing them, sir, wouldn't it be more natural to come up under plain sail?'

'Maybe, Mr Thomson, but I want quick manoeuvring when the time comes. You can shake the reefs out of the tops'ls, however, and make sure all's ready to crack on sail.'

At Thomson's low-voiced orders *Indefatigable*'s shrouds blackened with swarming men and her dingy canvas flapped and tautened. With the gusty wind just abaft the beam she sped lightly through the thickening twilight towards the pallid specks of sail ahead.

Another rocket shot aloft in a dwindling parabola. Jeremiah, motionless in his pea-jacket behind the silent gun-crews, watched it glumly, his thoughts on other things. That brief exchange between Paddon and the captain had revealed the gulf between him and them. The shared jest, the Christian name, the Latin words (he supposed them to be Latin or Greek) sealed these two as of that closed circle, the Gentry, which he was as yet far outside. He knew himself to be jealous of Paddon and was angry because of that; but he was angrier still that the boy's damning him for a clumsy lout had touched him on the raw.

Jeremiah had endured much from Mr Paddon in these past weeks and always with exemplary patience and good-humour, telling himself that this was the kind of thing he had expected, a test of temper and resolution that had to be passed. It had been less irksome because of something he found it hard to explain: despite Paddon's unfailing attitude of contempt and cold superiority Jeremiah felt a kindness for the boy, a curious emotion that seemed to embrace a vague sympathy for that attitude as well as regret that it prevented any friendly communication between them.

The sound of distant gunfire, a single cannon-shot, brought Jeremiah back to the immediate present.

'Admiral calling attention to his signal, I reckon, sir,' said Thomson at the taffrail above him.

'And by God it's needed!' said Bolton. 'Look at that, sir—larboard bow. A seventy-four and a three-decker going about and making a proper balls-up of it. They'll be on board of each other if they—'

'Mr Bell!' Pellew's voice cut in crisply. 'Carry my word along the deck, if you please. Gun-crews to stand down, hands ready at sheets and halliards, no talking. Full and bye, Mr Talley. Take the con and head straight in among 'em. Mr Packe, one rocket ready for firing.'

The fourth lieutenant passed along the deck repeating the order. Released from his action station, which had afforded him little view of *Indefatigable*'s progress, Jeremiah crossed the deck to the larboard rail just below the quarterdeck, where he was presently joined by the other four midshipmen. Night was closing in, but a waning moon above the low hurrying clouds shed light enough to show the remarkable scene. Stretching away on either bow was a confused mass of shipping, the nearest vessel a scant half-mile ahead of the frigate, big ships under reduced sail heading in all directions. Some had no lights, the poop lanterns of others struck sparks of yellow light from the crests of the choppy black seas.

'God, what a shambles!' commented Mr FitzJames professionally. 'Why don't Ned cut straight in and wallop 'em one after t'other?'

'Because he's no fool,' said Benedict, in the same careful undertone. 'There's thirty-two pounders among them that could blow a frigate out of the water with one discharge. The captain wants to preserve our incognito—that's why we're not closed up to the guns.'

'What'll he do, then? And what in the name of goodness are the French trying to do?'

'Get on a northerly course, seemingly,' observed Jeremiah, cupping his eyes with his hands the better to see. 'The three big uns on the beam are heading to cross our wake.'

'That's it, depend upon it,' Benedict said. 'De Galles was going to take his fleet out through the Raz, couldn't order his ships in time, and now he's trying the north passage—if he can make 'em understand what he—'

'Silence, you there!' grated the first lieutenant, above them.

At an order from Pellew the frigate's poop lantern flared into life. *Indefatigable* held steadily on, passing the first of the Frenchmen, a big frigate which had missed stays in coming about and was drifting with flapping sails, at half cannon-shot to larboard. A bawling of high-pitched voices drifted from her on the wind.

'Fire rocket,' snapped Pellew.

A hiss and a diminishing roar, and the thin bright column soaring from the quarter-deck lit a row of white faces along the rail of a French two-decker half-a-cable's length to starboard. A French voice yelled interrogatively and Pellew, muttering aside to Charles Paddon, waved his hat urgently in a gesture southward.

'*Le Raz!*' screeched Paddon. '*Le Raz de Sein! Au sud—au sud!*'

Then *Indefatigable* was past and in among the flock of scattered ships, firing her rockets at intervals with an occasional bang from the quarterdeck carronade to emphasise her meaningless signals, the master conning her deftly clear of the great hulls that loomed out of the darkness on either hand. When a blue radiance glowed suddenly far to larboard Pellew promptly sent two hands up the foreshrouds with blue-lights flaring. Doubtless the French lights indicated a prearranged code of night-signals, and if so he was bent on confusing them as much as possible. One result at least of his mischief was observed when a two-decker within musket-shot to larboard, sailing a parallel course with a transport too close on her beam, endeavoured to go about and collided with her companion so forcibly that her fore-topgallant mast snapped and crashed down into the transport's rigging.

Little of the ensuing turmoil on the decks of the two vessels could be seen in the windy darkness, but it could easily be imagined by *Indefatigable*'s hands, and their delighted ejaculations and thigh-slappings brought a reprimand from Thomson, whose shaky voice suggested stifled laughter.

Talley, beside the helm, had steered to take them well clear of the French ships they had passed so far and the first and only challenge came less than two minutes after that collision. They were approaching two ships moving slowly on the opposite course, with so small a space between them that the frigate had perforce to pass beam-to-beam with the larger of the two at thirty fathoms' distance. Jeremiah had to repress an inclination to duck as the mighty bowsprit, far above the level of *Indefatigable*'s quarterdeck, came thrusting out of the gloom. The Frenchman's towering side slid past opposite him, a smooth dark cliff on which he counted three tiers of closed gunports, and a voice from overhead hailed them querulously.

'*Quel vaisseau? Qu'est-ce que marche ici?*'

He heard Paddon reply that this was the *Masquerade*, out of Brest with dispatches for the Admiral, and then they were past and Pellew was leaning far out to scrutinize the mass of scroll-work and gilding dimly illuminated by her big stern-lantern.

'She's *Droits de l'Homme*, Mr Thomson.' There was something like awe in Pellew's tone. 'Eighty guns, thirty-two pounders—biggest they've got. If she's twigged us—'

He left the sentence unfinished. Captain and first lieutenant stared intently and somewhat anxiously after her. But the huge ship forged on steadily northward, with a brief gleam of moonshine turning her new canvas to silver.

'Sir!' said the master suddenly. 'Grand Stevenet on the starboard bow, and not half-a-league away!'

Indefatigable had passed through the main body of the French fleet and the black sea lay empty before her for two miles and more. At that distance ahead three white specks glimmered on the darkness: the last and southernmost three ships of De Galles' unwieldy armada. It was just possible to make out, beyond them, the long black bar of the land beween the sea and the faint luminosity of the sky. As Jeremiah knew, this was the southern arm of the bay, the big promontory running out from Douarnenez to the Pointe du Raz. Two of the three ships were well out on the frigate's larboard bow, the third coming up dead ahead, and to the right of his line-of-sight to the latter he could see a squat motionless blackness on the shifting waves, with the restless white gleam of broken water indicating the circle of sunken reefs. That, doubtless, was the Grand Stevenet.

Talley, summoned to the quarterdeck, was in urgent conference with captain and first lieutenant. Pellew sprang to the taffrail and rapped out orders.

'Away cutter's crew! Jump to it! Dowse that lantern, Mr Bell. Mr Coghlan, you'll take the cutter—'

'Let me go, sir,' broke in Paddon eagerly. 'I can handle—'

'Hold your tongue!' rasped Pellew. 'See if you can land on the rock yonder, Mr Coghlan. I want a rocket fired and three blue-lights lit and placed on the rock, visible to south'ard. Space 'em out as best you can. Mr Packe, you'll go in the cutter. Take two rockets and half-a-dozen blue-lights, flint, steel, tinder-box.'

Jeremiah turned to run amidships. The captain's voice arrested him.

'You've thirty minutes, Mr Coghlan. Not a second more.'

3

The cutter swayed and twisted as the swirl between the rock-reefs took hold of her hull. In the sternsheets grey-headed Mr Packe, the tarpaulin bag containing his combustibles between his knees, wrestled with the tiller. Jeremiah stood erect in the bows holding the long boathook, gesturing to larboard or starboard with his free hand and peering earnestly for the next patch of smooth jet-black water. The cutter's crew, who had pulled the half-mile from *Indefatigable*'s side in something under five minutes, were urging her less lustily now that she was in among the rocks that defended Grand Stevenet on the west.

Jeremiah had made his approach on that side to get a lee from the wind, and from the corner of his eye as he conned her in he could see the small white blur of the approaching ship on his right hand; fortunately she was coming up slowly, no doubt under reefed topsails. Astern the frigate lay hove-to, invisible in the darkness unless one knew where to look for her. Ahead, now hardly a biscuit-toss away, Grand Stevenet reared, a black mass shaped like a crouching lion. The sliding white glint at its base suggested ledges there to an eye accustomed to night-groping into rocky smuggling coves. That, he supposed, was why Pellew had picked him for this mad venture. Perhaps not so mad, though, not such an unlikely chance when you consider the French captain, puzzled maybe by the reversal of orders and mazed by unintelligible rockets and flares. The odds were he'd make for a vessel showing signal lights to find out the facts of the matter, and then—

'Bottom 'ere,' said someone.

The boat lurched as the larboard oars scraped underwater rock. Jeremiah sounded with his boathook and found half-a-fathom. Grand Stevenet towered close above him, its base twenty or thirty feet away.

'Way enough,' he said. 'Hold her and fend off. Mr Packe, I'll take the fireworks.'

'You get along,' said Packe placidly, at his elbow. 'A run ashore'll do me good.'

Jeremiah got overside into icy water and braced himself with the boathook while he lent a hand to the gunner; no time for argument, with only thirty minutes allowed him. (*Thirty minutes, lad*; Abner Best's voice—only four weeks ago?—came oddly to mind.) He slid and stumbled through a swirl of water, kneedeep or waist-deep as the waves came surging round the rock, Packe close behind him with the tarpaulin bag slung round his neck. His hands slithered on smooth wet rock, found hold in a crack lined with barnacles, and with a grunt and heave he was sprawling on a slanting ledge, just sufficiently firmly established to bring Packe up with a strong haul. Six feet higher a shelf of drier rock gave them fair standing-room and some shelter from the wind. Above this shelf rose the main wall of the rock, sheer and slimy with seagull-droppings. Packe unslung his bag.

'Rocket from here?' he shouted above the wash and grumble of waves.

'Yes. Quick as you can. And give me the blue-lights.'

Jeremiah stuffed the blue-lights into his shirt—he was soaked nearly to the armpits—while the gunner set up the folding wooden firing-frame and placed the rocket so that it pointed clear of the rock-wall and into the wind. Flint and steel scraped once, twice, three times. Tinder flamed briefly and the fuse spluttered into life.

Up soared the rocket with a rush and a stink, and before it had reached the peak of its windblown parabola Jeremiah had seized flint and tinder and was edging leftward along the shelf. It sloped upward, narrowing as it went, and in ten feet had brought him to a spot where only careful balance prevented him from pitching backwards onto half-seen rocks below.

A blind grope round a corner found him a projecting pinnacle to swing on and he landed awkwardly in a cleft on the windward end of the Stevenet, between (as it were) the lion's paws. A quick glance southward showed the white sail nearer and apparently heading to pass east of the rock. He jammed the wooden handle of a blue-light into a crack at waist-level and shielding his tinder from the gusty wind as best he could struck a light at last.

The touch-paper caught but smouldered dubiously. Cupping his hands round it to encourage the red glow resulted in searing agony when the bright flare sprang up, but he clambered swiftly on round the slimy blocks and bastions of the lion's south flank with a ghastly blue glare lighting his way, oblivious of the pain.

Twenty feet along he came to a stand. On this side of the rock the black waves surged and foamed at the base of flat-topped bollards cleft by narrow cracks, making progress easy enough until they ended abruptly in a sheer and vertical face. No possible way onward there. Above his head the crag lay back a little in glistening bulges, and at his feet a suitable crevice showed in the pillar-top he was standing on. He rammed a blue-light into it and after half-a-dozen failures succeeded in lighting it.

Anxiety lest he should be seen from the French ship's deck filled his mind and gave extra impulse to his desperate climb up the slime-covered bulges with toes slipping and fingers finding fortuitous hold in the nick of time. The slanting and luckily narrow spine of the Stevenet was clutched at last and he got an arm and then a leg over it, sitting astride with the wind whipping his hair across his face. A ridge below his thigh—the edge of a crack, and just where it was needed. One blue-light directly above another would suggest that they were hung in a ship's shrouds. The crack was just too wide for the wooden handle but he wedged it with his handkerchief, placing it so that it would be shielded from the wind by his body. The pain of his hands rendered the striking of flint and steel difficult, and when at length the short fuse caught it sputtered damply and he had again to protect it with his palms and endure a second brief spell of torment when it burst into flame.

The glare and drifting smoke from the lights between him and the Frenchman allowed him no sight of her. Would that glare light the shape of the rock for the men on board her, or would it spoil their night-sight so that they could imagine the Grand Stevenet a ship hove-to? Would she try to come within hailing distance or pass by? How far out did the shoals on the south of the Stevenet extend?

Jeremiah remembered that at least half of his allotted time must have expired and looked to his descent. No going back by the way he had come, and the north flank of the rock, sheer and black and featureless to his dazzled eyes, offered no hope of getting down that he could see.

'Aloft there!' came Packe's voice above the groan and slap of the waves. 'How are ye fixed?'

Packe was a yard or two to westward of him and maybe fifteen feet below, on the ledge where he had been left.

'I'll have to slide, like as not,' Jeremiah called down to him. 'Stand by to grapple me.'

He shuffled along *à cheval* until he was directly above the gunner and contrived to lower himself to arm's length with the aid of the convenient crack. His foot found precarious hold in the cleft behind a detached flake and one hand grasped its razor-sharp edge, but a second later the foothold failed him and he flew downward, his head striking the rock-edge as he fell. There was a yowk from Packe as he took the shock, but he gripped Jeremiah by arm and collar and pinned him to the floor of the shelf. Without a word they scrambled down to the base of the lion's plinth and into the wash of the waves, Jeremiah with his rescued boathook and Packe with his bag. Both were drenched to the neck before helping hands lugged them over the gunwale into the cutter's bows.

'We can put about 'ere, sir,' said a voice.

'Right.' Jeremiah stood up with his boathook ready for fending off. 'Handsomely, now. Tiller over, Mr Packe. Give way, all.'

Slowly and deviously the cutter drew out into deep water, again holding to the lee side of the Grand Stevenet. Jeremiah made out, with some difficulty, the ghostly shape of the frigate hovering in the darkness beyond half-a-mile of sea to northward, but as soon as the boat was clear of the shoals he turned to watch the strange scene astern of him.

The black lion-shape of the Grand Stevenet was in silhouette against a pallid blue radiance, a startling brilliance still between dark sky and darker sea though the blue-lights were dimming now to their end. Spectrally illuminated, though distantly, a big ship was closing in towards the Stevenet, the white wave at her forefoot and her white topsails reflecting the fading glare and her massive hull a shadowy but still distinguishable mass.

'A seventy-four, by God!' muttered Packe.

She came on. No one else spoke. The oarsman stopped pulling and rested on their oars unreprimanded, watching open-mouthed. A moment of breathless anticipation prolonged itself inordinately. Then, a cable's length out from the big rock, she struck. They heard the grinding crash clearly above the noise of the sea, saw her foretopmast lean and plunge across her beak-head, clean broken at the cap and dragging the main royal and topgallant spars after it; heard, too, a thin babel of human voices borne briefly on a gust of wind. Jeremiah swallowed hard and thought of the wreckers he had heard of down Penzance way. He had always loathed their trade and now he was one of them. For the first time he was conscious of the fierce smart of his burned hands and of the warm wet stream that trickled down his cheek and under his shirt. He lugged off his neckcloth and mopped angrily at the blood.

'Oars!' he cried harshly. 'Give way, and put your guts into it!'

Ten minutes later he was in the captain's cabin on board *Indefatigable*, dripping seawater onto the coir matting and making his report. Pellew, his lean red face alive with triumph, heard him out without interruption.

'They'll get her off,' he said at the end, 'but she'll not put to sea for a week or two. One less for their damned expedition, wherever it's bound—and a dozen to come, please God, when our line-of-battles get after 'em. Now get Mr Tierney to clap a plaster on that cut and bandage your hands. You did well, Mr Coghlan—very well.'

4

But God, it seemed, did not please. The *Séduisant*, 74 (it was months later when the frigate's people learned her name) was to be the only enemy ship disabled on the outward passage of Admiral de Galles' invasion fleet.

Indefatigable won clear of Camaret Bay without difficulty or incident, beating east and then north across the Goulette entrance to run through the night close in to the bay's northern shores and steal out past the familiar dangers of Pointe St Mathieu. In worsening weather she thrashed her way to the rendezvous, and there beat up and down for twenty-four hours before *Revolutionnaire* hove in sight. Captain Cole had spent a day quartering the seas where the offshore squadron was supposed to be and had failed to find Sir John Colpoys and his ten ships of the line.

If Pellew doubted the efficiency of Cole's search he said nothing of it. Leaving *Revolutionnaire* to keep watch off Ushant, he drove his ship through the easterly gales to find Colpoys himself. In fair visibility a masthead lookout could see to the perimeter of a circle of nine miles radius. Doubling his lookouts by day and firing guns and rockets by night, he proved to his own satisfaction that Sir John was not on his station nor within a hundred miles of it.

Some unforeseen happening, he thought, must have forced the rear-admiral to take his ships back to Falmouth, or—less probably—he had conjectured De Galles' intention to be the invasion of Portugal, Britain's one remaining ally, and had sailed for Coruna to intercept him. Pellew, knowing only too well his senior's habit of mind, decided for Falmouth. There being nothing more he could do with two frigates cut off from their parent squadron, he headed *Indefatigable* and *Revolutionnaire* for the Channel, smouldering with anger and frustration at the lost chance. His ship's company shared his sentiments.

'It's a thrice-damned copper-bottomed bloody shame,' declared Midshipman Delamere, ducking into the lantern-lit cockpit and tossing his wet tarpaulin on the deck. 'If the Reverend Benedict wasn't present I'd put it stronger.'

Benedict looked up from the book he was peering into. 'You can't put it too strongly for me, Del,' he said. 'All the same, philosophical calm's the only remedy in this situation. In my opinion—'

'To hell with philosophical calm!' said Delamere. 'It don't help us to beat the French.'

He sat down heavily beside Jeremiah, who was hunched over the table with a pencil awkwardly held in his bandaged hand, working a problem in spherical trigonometry.

'Here we are off the Manacles,' he went on exasperatedly. 'Falmouth Bay in an hour, the Fleet in port and Colpoys God knows where, while the Frogs are out and away on some devil's business without a Navy ship to stop 'em.'

There was no denying it. In a glum silence the hollow roar of the seas rushing along the frigate's side sounded derisive, and the squeak of the lantern on its deckhead hook made mocking comment. Jeremiah saw Charles Paddon's face peering from the bunk where he was lying and remembered that the boy had not addressed him once since his return from the Grand Stevenet. How Paddon must have winced under that public rebuke when he had—young fool!—interrupted Pellew's orders! And how he must writhe at the knowledge that Coghlan the fisherman's son, the clumsy lout, had once again won credit that was denied to him! There was no satisfaction in the thought, only an understanding—strangely painful—of what Paddon must be feeling. He pushed it out of his mind.

'Where would you say the French fleet's bound for, Ben?' he asked.

'I've told you. Portugal, beyond a doubt. Now Spain's sold herself to the Directory, France controls every base on the Atlantic coast except the Portuguese ports. It stands to reason De Galles was ordered to go for Coruna and Lisbon soon as he could get to sea.' Benedict gestured emphatically with *The Rights of Man*, in which he had inserted a finger to mark his place. 'In my opinion Sir John Colpoys resolved likewise and has gone after them. Doubtless he—'

'Stuff,' interrupted Delamere loudly. 'Colpoys wouldn't take his ships after pussy if pussy was twice his own force, let alone three or four times. Any wine in that mug of yours, Jerry?'

Jeremiah pushed the half-empty mug across

to him. The big midshipman nodded thanks and took a gulp.

'No,' he continued. 'Ask me, and I'll tell you they're bound for Ireland. My father was over on his estate in County Cork last month and he says the country's hotching with rebels—United Irishmen, National Volunteers in French uniforms, secret musters under arms, God knows what-all. If they get a footing there—but what's the use of ifs? There's but one certainty, and that's that they'll be short of one seventy-four.' He raised his mug. 'Jerry, I drink to you—the only reefer that ever knocked the spars off an enemy ship with fireworks.'

'That's what they call blarney in Ireland,' said Jeremiah. ''Twas Captain Pellew took the trick.'

'With J. Coghlan for trump card,' said Delamere. 'Well, I'm for forty minutes' doss.'

He heaved himself into his bunk. Benedict resumed his book. Jeremiah caught a glimpse of Paddon's thin handsome face, dark eyes gleaming resentfully, before it withdrew into the shadows. Nothing here was his fault and Charles Paddon's behaviour was eminently unreasonable—and yet he felt pity, even affection, for the boy. That was odd. He fumbled painfully for his pencil and applied himself with an inward sigh, to spherical trigonometry.

CHAPTER FOUR

THE RIGHTS OF MAN

1

'Fastest bloody turnround a ship ever made.' This was the verdict of *Indefatigable*'s crew, half rueful and half admiring, on her proceedings at Falmouth. It was a true verdict. The two frigates berthed under the guns of Pendennis Castle, where *Amazon* was already lying, in the morning of December 19th; by noon of December 20th Pellew's squadron of three vessels was heading out again past the Point into the windswept greyness of the Channel.

There was no shore leave for any man. Before *Indefatigable*'s cable had finished roaring out through the hawse-hole Pellew was off in the cutter with his second lieutenant, and in an incredibly short time the water-hoys and ammunition barges were alongside. All hands—midshipmen and petty officers as well—worked at the hauling and stowing under Thomson's relentless supervision. Casks of water, biscuit, salt meat, were trundled along the deck and below in unceasing thunder, processions of men carried powder-barrels and shot for the eighteen- and twenty-four-pounders. Lower-deck rumour placed the bribe with which Sir Edward had spurred the dockyard to this unprecedented promptness at anything from a hundred to a thousand guineas.

'He's a fly 'un, is the cap'n,' panted bosun's mate Camden, hauling next to Jeremiah Coghlan on the falls of the mainyard tackle. 'Used this new-fangled tallygraft, Noakes o' the cutter's crew says. Message all the way to Portsmouth afore a man can say Jack Robinson.'

Pellew had indeed taken advantage of the semaphore telegraph to inform Admiral Lord Bridport of the French fleet's escape from Brest. He had also sent a long dispatch, post, to Admiralty in London, setting forth the situation as he saw it and his immediate intentions. Colpoys's squadron had not returned to Falmouth; therefore Sir John had either been blown far off his station by the easterly gales or had made for Coruna to intercept the French. He, Pellew, would proceed at once to Coruna with two frigates, leaving the third stationed off Ushant, the original rendezvous appointed by Colpoys. Having cleared his yardarm thus he could turn to more tasks of immediate urgency; conference with Cole of *Revolutionnaire* and Reynolds of *Amazon*, drafting of orders, receipts of reports from lieutenants, boatswain, gunner and purser, and a dozen other matters. To the best of Midshipman Coghlan's knowledge his captain took no sleep or rest in that twenty-four hours at Falmouth. By now Edward Pellew had eclipsed all other heroes in Jeremiah's eyes; he had attained almost the status of a god.

Revolutionnaire and *Amazon*, with *Indefatigable* leading them, took their departure from Lizard Point in the last light of December 20th, a day of shifting winds and confused seas. Next day *Revolutionnaire* detached herself in obedience to Pellew's signal-gun and hoist and turned south for her station off Ushant with a strengthening nor'-westerly gale to speed her on her way. The two remaining frigates held on south by west for Cape Ortegal and Coruna. Twice in that 500-mile passage they had to lie-to for a day under close-reefed maintopsails only, while the hungry green seas smashed over beakhead and weather bow and a storm-force nor'-wester hammered them mercilessly.

It was Christmas Day before Cape Ortegal was sighted, a Christmas Day marked only by double grog and seasonable jocularities between spells at the pumps. And from now on, while *Indefatigable* cruised southward with her consort down the coast of Portugal, the wintry gales persisted, the wind shifting between west and north-west with rare and brief lulls between the shifts.

They seemed to have the tossing seas to themselves. Of French armada or pursuing

British squadron there was no sign, and when early in the new year of 1797 Pellew came upon a solitary storm-tossed merchantman venturing the passage from Lisbon to Oporto her Portuguese captain could tell him only that nothing had been heard of any French invasion fleet on that coast. Three weeks had gone by since De Galles sailed from Brest; his armada could have been off Coruna in four days. Had the Biscay storms driven him to seek shelter in St Nazaire or La Rochelle? And was Colpoys blockading him there?

Pellew turned northward and began the long beat back again, his masthead lookouts relieved every hour in the bitter weather. For the officers and men of his deck-watches there was no respite until the four double strokes of the bell that meant that they could throw themselves into bunk or hammock and rest their drenched and weary bodies. Whenever gun-drill was remotely possible the eighteen-pounders of the upper deck and the twenty-four-pounders of the main deck were cast loose from their double breechings and the gun-crews exercised. When *Indefatigable* was heeled too far over in a heavy blow for the guns to be run out the topmen were exercised aloft, and with the topmen went the midshipmen. Chilled to the bone, with the gale tearing savagely at their bodies, they clawed their way to the topgallant jacks, out along the yards, back and down—and up again to repeat the perilous journey. At this game Jeremiah was a match for all but the most experienced topman and revelled in the race aloft and the fight with the snatching gale, but he was soon aware that for Charles Paddon every such exercise held the terror of anticipated death.

Paddon, who was in Jeremiah's watch, was as alert for the captain's sudden roar as Jeremiah himself and as prompt in jumping to the shrouds, so that more often than not his pale strained face was a foot beneath Jeremiah's heels as they clambered up the futtocks and his desperate clutchings and clawings manifest when it came to edging out along the footropes. Once, when Paddon's long thin fingers missed a frantic grasp, Jeremiah yelled the old sea precept at him.

'One hand for the ship and one for yourself, man!'

But there was no sign that he had been heard. The boy's fear was so acute that Jeremiah seemed to feel it communicated to his own inner self. And yet when he had climbed shakily down to the deck Paddon never said a word or gave a sign that admitted the ordeal he had faced. It was impossible not to admire his courage. Jeremiah found himself contriving to keep close to Paddon in these aerial manoeuvres; and wondered at the impulse that set him watching, like a hen with a chick, over a lad whose aloof contempt persisted in all their intercourse.

Forty leagues nor'-nor'-west of Finisterre, the gale moderating, the frigates spoke a Portuguese brig. With some peril to himself her captain came on board, with a tale to tell that brought elucidation of Pellew's problem. A fierce gale had driven his brig almost into Dunmanus Bay on the Irish coast on Christmas Day, and he had sighted a great fleet heading north that same afternoon. Ireland! Morard de Galles and his ships and soldiers had been bound for the invasion of Ireland after all. By now they could have united with the Irish rebels—by now they could have landed 15,000 troops in Pembroke or Somerset, with nothing but militia and half-trained yeomanry between them and London.

Indefatigable and *Amazon* thrashed on northward, under the maximum sail they could bear in such weather. January 13th, dawning as dark and stormy as any of the preceding days, found them somewhere west of Ushant, their position uncertain because the noon sights of the past four days had been little better than guesswork. *Amazon*, a league or more astern, was invisible from *Indefatigable*'s spray-swept, steep-tilted deck. At noon a seaman came staggering aft along the lifeline to strike eight bells at the belfry abaft the wheel, and the afternoon watch tumbled-up in their tarpaulins.

By tacit permission of the captain the midshipmen of the watch had established their right to ensconce themselves, when the gale blew too strong for exercise, in what Delamere called 'the shooting box', which was the corner of the weather rail immediately below the taffrail of the quarterdeck. Here they could stand or squat with a lee from the volleying spray that swept overhead, within earshot of their commander's orders and yet able to talk among themselves. Pellew, who had been unusually withdrawn and irritable during these weeks of anxiety and frustration, liked having his side of the quarterdeck to himself with only his senior officers within call, and when the first lieutenant objected to the midshipmen's practice had snubbed Thomson sharply.

The westerly gale had freshened steadily throughout the morning and the frigate, with the gale on her beam, was lying over so steeply on the gigantic swell that gun-drill and exercise aloft were both out of the question. The young gentlemen of the afternoon watch, trooping aft with one eye on the quarterdeck, received no notice from their seniors and huddled into their shooting-box; Benedict, Delamere, Coghlan and Paddon had their pea-jackets buttoned to the neck and their hats jammed over their eyes.

They pressed themselves against the shuddering planking and resumed the debate which Benedict had initiated over their lunch of biscuit and small beer. Some mention of the senior midshipman's favourite philosopher had prompted Delamere (more in mischief than in earnest) to denounce Tom Paine as an ally of the Jacobins and a bloody liar. Benedict took up his interrupted argument with a heat that defied the bitter cold.

'I say it again, Del!' He had to shout above the continuous uproar of wind and sea. 'That's the libel of every shallow-pated ass. Paine's the ally of no country—he's the ally of humanity. In my opinion he's the one man to see clear ahead when the rest of us are staring at our own noses.'

'Damn your opinion!' Delamere shouted back. 'Take a stare at the facts, man. Your friend Mr Bloody Paine 'listed with the American rebels, didn't he? Now he's with those murdering blackguards in Paris. You can pitch your rights of man into the drink, Ben—no man's a right to fight against his king and country.'

He squeezed back under the bulwarks as a wave-top slashed at the rail and flung a spout of seawater down the slope of the deck.

'I'm not saying the Jacobins and the Johnny Rebs are in the right,' Benedict countered loudly. 'I'm saying Tom Paine's got hold of the truth. War won't hammer the truth into thick skulls like yours—you've got to see it and admit it. Then we'll get justice, then we'll get—'

'Justice being the little man coming up and the big man coming down, I take it.'

'Precisely!' cried Benedict defiantly. 'What's your big man? A tyrant who's in power because his father was in power. The veriest clod-poll can settle the fate of his fellow-men because of his name and his money, while a thousand more able men are kept down in the mud at his feet.'

'Where they belong,' Delamere growled.

'No man belongs in the mud!' Benedict turned to Jeremiah, who was squatting beside him. 'You'll support me, Jerry?'

'Well, I don't know,' Jeremiah said slowly. 'I'd sooner King George had his bottom on the throne than me. Wind's still freshening,' he added, as a fiercer gust pushed the frigate over and set them all clutching at the belaying-pin rack along the rail.

'That's not the point. Look at this, now. Two women are giving birth—'

Thomson's bellow cut short this interesting statement. 'Reef courses! One reef in fore, main and mizzen!'

Petty officers came skittering along the lifelines yelling the orders, the deck swarmed and emptied as the hands clambered up the shrouds. The four midshipmen were clinging their way up the stiff wet cordage of the rigging before the shouting had ceased, Paddon close below Jeremiah. Edging out along the footrope of the mizzen yard with the gale doing its best to tear them from their hold, tugging with numbed fingers at the flapping canvas, they tied their reef-knots and scuttled down again through drenching spray to the shelter of the shooting-box.

'She rides easier already,' Jeremiah commented, cramming his big form into the meagre cover of the rail.

Benedict, after a minute to recover his breath, took up his proposition where he had left it. 'Two women have babies—'

'Not guilty, my lord,' Delamere interjected, and was ignored.

'—one woman's a duchess, the other's a labourer's wife. Both boys. Those babies come out into the world equal, naked, not a groat to choose between them. That stands to reason. Change 'em over a second after they're born and the labourer's son will make as good a duke as—'

'Ignorant rubbish!'

The interruption came from Charles Paddon. The others regarded him with some surprise; Paddon usually held himself aloof from their debates.

'Any man of sense knows it's rubbish you're talking,' he went on heatedly. 'I'll not stand by and hear it, Benedict! You've never read history—or your Bible—if you credit such nonsense. All experience shows that the rulers of men are born, not made. You'll not deny there's such a thing as royal blood, I hope?'

'No,' returned Benedict, recovering from his astonishment. 'But I deny that it gives a man the right to rule. It's other qualities—'

'Right!' cried Paddon shrilly, with a sneer. 'You're precious ready with your rights, but there's such a thing as duty. The blood in his veins, the blood of kings—centuries, generations of it—makes a man the proper ruler of his fellows. It's the duty of other men to recognise it.'

'Oh ballocks, young Paddon!' said Delamere, changing sides. 'What of Charlie Stuart's four dozen bastards? Did Charlie's blood make 'em all rulers?'

'It gave them all the right to rule!' riposted Paddon, his dark eyes flashing.

Benedict spoke hotly. 'So because a fellow's great-great-grandfather has a dram of some bygone tyrant's blood he's to trample on the rest of us—that's your contention? I'll tell you what Paine says about that. "The vanity and presumption of governing beyond the grave is the most ridiculous of all tyrannies." Now that, in my opinion—'

'Pipe down, Ben!' Jeremiah broke in harshly.

They fell silent, listening. Again the faint high call came from the masthead.

'Deck! On deck, there! Sail, fine o' the stabboard bow!'

Captain Pellew came jumping down from the

quarterdeck to run for'ard and up the foremast shrouds. In the reeling foretop he steadied his glass as best he could and at last caught and held the far grey speck that appeared and disappeared among the waves ahead. A big ship—a very big ship—heading sou'west across his own course. A straggler from De Galles' armada? It could be. He watched a moment longer and then clambered down and ran aft.

'Mr Thomson, bear away two points, if you please.'

'Hands to the braces!' roared Thomson. 'Starboard helm—steady as you go!'

Indefatigable reeled and plunged with the wind over her larboard quarter, while every glass on her quarterdeck scanned the grey-green wastes of heaving water. In a very short time the three masts and their upper sails could be seen ahead when the frigate rose on a crest.

'French line of battle, or I'm a Dutchman,' said Thomson.

Pellew's sharp orders followed instantly on the first lieutenant's words. With a smile on his lean face and a new spring in his step, he went below to record the start of an action soon to be famous throughout Britain.

'*The wind was then at West blowing hard, with thick hazey Weather. I instantly made the signal to the* Amazon *for a General Chace & follow'd it by the signal that the Chace was an Enemy.*'

2

As often as one of the wallowing green sea-mountains lifted *Indefatigable* Jeremiah could see the enemy. The huge vessel was well within long gunshot on the larboard bow, rolling and spouting like a giant whale as she rose, sinking into the troughs until her deck was hidden from him. That deck was crowded with people, many of them soldiers judging by the masses of green and light blue. If ever she succeeded in boarding the odds against the frigate would be something like four to one, he guessed; and, more certainly, she had three times *Indefatigable*'s gun-power. Only the fact that she was to windward, heeling over so steeply that her lower-deck gunports were under water and the others necessarily closed, kept those 32-pounders from hammering her smaller adversary.

It was two bells of the first dogwatch and the dark January day was drawing to its close. It had taken the frigate five hours to come to these close quarters, risking main courses and topsails under a reefed-topsail gale, for the big Frenchman had spread extra canvas when she saw her pursuer. *Amazon* was out of sight astern. Jeremiah himself could not have identified the French ship, but Captain Pellew had done so with assurance and that was good enough for him. She was the *Droits de l'Homme*, the three-decker whose towering flank they had so nearly scraped that night in Camaret Bay four stormy weeks ago. The coincidence of her name with Benedict's half-baked argument (and Paddon's self-revealing refutation) crossed his mind but was banished by a sudden roar from the quarterdeck and the ensuing *rafale* of the drums beating to quarters.

Every man had been waiting for this the past hour and more and the gun-crews were at their stations in a matter of seconds. Jeremiah, balancing against the tilt and sway of the deck in rear of his two 24-pounders, divined his captain's intention and marvelled at it; Pellew was going to cross the enemy's stern and rake her. For a single frigate to attack an 80-gun ship was an unheard-of thing—and yet, with half the Frenchman's guns impotent, there was reason in it.

'Starboard broadside only!' yelled Gaze, who had charge of it. 'All guns run out!'

The howl of the wind, the roaring wash of the seas, almost drowned the hollow rumble of the gun-trucks. Another bellowed order and up the shrouds raced the hands from the larboard side to trice up the main courses. *Indefatigable* swung her bows to larboard and plunged close-hauled across the big ship's wake.

'On the upward roll!' came Gaze's shout. 'Fire as your guns bear!'

Jeremiah found himself looking up at the

massive gilded stern of the *Droits de l'Homme*, so close that he could see the levelled muskets of the men who crowded along the poop rail. The ripple of bright flame and the splatter of shots came an instant before the frigate's for'ard guns opened fire, initiating an almost continuous din of deafening explosions, so fast was *Indefatigable* passing her target. The dazzling brilliance of the orange flashes emphasised the fast-falling darkness.

She was past and turning to starboard before he could see what damage, if any, they had done—and now the French captain saw and took his chance. He put his helm down, yawing to larboard so that the rows of open gunports in his ship's windward side fronted *Indefatigable* as she drew abreast.

Jeremiah flung himself forward to help the gun-crews as they struggled to run out their reloaded guns, but the French broadside blazed and thundered before the muzzles were through the ports. A shriek higher than the voice of the wind passed overhead—most of the shot was aimed high—but in the same instant the frigate leapt and shuddered to the impact of several balls on her hull.

'Ready—ready,' came the shouts along the deck as the gun-captains reported.

'All guns, fire!'

Gaze, having to fire with the lee-side guns, had waited for the upward roll as she soared on a crest and had gauged his moment accurately. Main and fore topmasts bent and crashed to the Frenchman's deck, to the sound of a breathless cheer from the British gunners.

'Reload! Reload! And lively!' screeched Gaze, racing along behind the guns.

In yawing for that broadside *Droits de l'Homme* had lost way and *Indefatigable* was drawing ahead, and if Pellew could cross her bows he could again rake her with his starboard broadside, from stem to stern. The frigate had begun her turn to starboard when the Frenchman altered course again. Her captain, whoever he was, wasted no opportunities; a good fighting seaman, Jeremiah decided.

Droits de l'Homme came foaming down on a converging course like a charging bull, aiming to close and board. He saw the plunging beakhead loom through a cloud of flying spray, heard Pellew's voice, sharp with urgency, barking orders; felt the frigate tilt and swing below him; and then they were rushing past on the opposite course, the high wooden flank with its smoking gunports no more than half pistol-shot away. Musketry crackled briefly overhead. A ball thudded into the planking between Jeremiah's feet and a man from the crew of Number 9 gun gave a yell and crumpled to the deck.

'Got me leg, the bleedin' sods,' he gasped as the midshipman dragged him clear of the traces.

Two loblolly-boys came running at Jeremiah's hail to carry him below and as they lifted him *Droits de l'Homme* fired her broadside again, eight hundredweight of murderous iron that could have blasted the frigate into splinters if it had hit her. As it was, *Indefatigable* was clear by a second of time and not a shot took effect; nor—so swiftly had the two vessels passed—had her larboard gun-crews had a chance to fire. When she could make easterly again *Droits de l'Homme* was far ahead. Reports were coming aft to the captain now.

'Carpenter, sir—two shot 'oles abaft the mainmast, above waterline. Party plugging 'em now.'

'Mr Tierney's respecks, sir, an' we've three wounded, none serious, an' no killed.'

'Boatswain here, sir. Crossjack slings parted, foreshrouds all to blazes on the stabb'd side, outer jib halyard—'

'Sir! Sir!' Bell came rushing aft. '*Amazon*, coming up fast!'

In the heat of the manoeuvring and firing *Amazon*'s approach had not been observed and she was already hull-up. She came flying over the darkening rollers under a press of sail that seemed likely to thrust her bowsprit-first under the heaving surface, a vengeful beauty.

The signal for close action was at *Indefatigable*'s yardarm as she passed but

Robert Reynolds knew his senior captain's mind and needed no signal. They watched her race on, heeled far over, bucking through the charging seas, and saw her broadside blaze out as she crossed the Frenchman's quarter. Then she was gone into the grey gloom, her spread of canvas driving her past *Droits de l'Homme*. Wind and sea had now risen to such a pitch that the best of sea-officers would think twice before putting his ship about.

Indefatigable, with urgent rigging repairs to be done and a 24-pounder ball in her mainmast, made sail to pass well to leeward of the Frenchman and come up with her consort. By now night had fallen and in the spray-swept darkness the boatswain's party spliced and rigged, and the carpenter and his mate crawled up to assess the damage to the mainmast, while the three ships swept on eastward before the gale, the frigates well in advance of the battleship. In relays the hands were sent below to supper; biscuits, salt meat and grog—a cold supper for men chilled and soaked, but the galley-fire had been doused when they cleared for action. At eight bells of the last dogwatch *Indefatigable* and *Amazon* separated and prepared to re-engage the enemy.

And now began a grim hunting through night and storm. The howling of the wind had given place to the eldritch shriek of a hurricane, and there could be no manoeuvring for position.

The frigates placed themselves one on either bow of the *Droits de l'Homme* within gunshot, firing whenever their guns would bear; and by yawing to one side or the other the battleship contrived to return their fire with interest.

Indefatigable being on the Frenchman's starboard bow, her larboard guns did all the firing and Jeremiah and his men spent most of that wild night racing up and down the shrouds to make or reduce sail. He could not sufficiently admire the superb seamanship that kept the frigate in her aggressive position and nursed her in a storm that seemed every moment about to snap her tall masts and end her career for ever.

The wind blew the gunsmoke clear at once after every discharge and by the intermittent glare, reflected from the hurtling backs of monster waves, it was possible to get glimpses of the Frenchman's deck. Half her starboard rail had gone and there were dead men and wounded there; her sails were riddled with shot and her two outer jibs had gone. Yet she surged on with no slackening of her fire, an angry bull harassed by snapping hounds.

Indefatigable's sails, too, were full of shot-holes, and the red-painted table in her cockpit, where Mr Tierney was hard at work, would need scrubbing before the young gentlemen sat round it again.

Hour after hour the three ships drove on through the roaring seas, dwarfed by toppling black waves, tossed high on foaming crests that broke across their decks, firing on the merest glimpse of an adversary in the heaving chaos. In *Indefatigable* there was no respite for officers or crew. Rarely though the Frenchman's intermittent gunnery took effect there were wounded spars and wounded men to be tended and deck litter to be cleared, and a 32-pounder ball that smashed into the frigate's quarter added to the amount of water in her holds. Down on her maindeck the men were up to their thighs in swilling water and all but two of the guns were out of action. The pumps began their ceaseless clanking, manned by seamen, midshipmen and petty officers in relays organised by Gaze.

Jeremiah, taking his spell with the rest, found himself toiling next to Charles Paddon at the iron handle. The smoky light from a wildly-swinging lantern showed Paddon's face, the clenched jaw and the sparkle of dark eyes; excitement, even joy of battle, were there. The boy's got guts, right enough, thought Jeremiah, and felt again that odd spasm of pride and liking which a father might feel for a son. Yet when he ventured a nod and a grin at his neighbour—the deafening uproar below decks made conversation impossible—Paddon only frowned and concentrated on the work.

A gust of cheering sounded on the upper deck when he staggered up the ladder at the end of his spell. Caldecott, clinging his way for'ard along the lifeline with a message, paused to shout that they'd hit the Frenchman's mizzen. A minute later the glare from her guns showed him the ruin of mast and spars and flapping sails, with antlike figures swarming to clear it before the following seas could broach her to. A more distant flash, briefly silhouetting jagged wave-tops, told that *Amazon* still kept up her harassing fire. Then a yell and a rush of men swept him up the shrouds to take another reef in the mizzen topsail.

There was no sign of the gale's moderating. Rather it seemed to increase about two o'clock in the morning, and so violent became the tossing of the frigate that one of the maindeck guns on the lee side drew the ringbolts out of the planking and went splashing and trundling to and fro across the deck, aimless death let loose. Jeremiah was with the party that dodged and grabbed futilely to trap the monster, but it was Pellew, leaving the quarterdeck for the first time in nine hours, who directed its final ensnaring with the aid of piled hammocks. And after that came the long business of double-securing all the inactive guns by reeving endless fathoms of spare cordage; two tons of iron rolling down a 45-degree slope could smash a hole in the ship's side, let alone maim horribly a man who got in its way.

On and on through the black fury of the

storm, firing, reloading, firing again when the *Droits de l'Homme* showed briefly in the windy darkness, they pitched and wallowed eastward. Pellew had spilled his wind so as to let *Indefatigable* drop astern of the Frenchman, and now they were pounding her quarterdeck. *Amazon*, after a while perceiving the manoeuvre, fell back also to fire on her larboard quarter.

Eight bells of the middle watch, and mugs and pannikins of rum were served out from a cask on deck. As he gulped the mouthful of liquor Jeremiah gave a thought to the chart. Did Captain Pellew know anything at all of their position? Somewhere east of them was the long mainland of France, the dangerous Biscay coast, and it seemed to him that they had been racing eastward for days. There was a hidden moon above the dismal cloud-rack overhead, giving light enough to discern *Droits de l'Homme* thrashing through mountains and valleys of seething water, her canvas in rags and her cordage streaming loose-ended before the gale. Delamere, draining a pannikin at his side, yelled in his ear.

'Short shrift now for Ben's rights of man!'

But still she fired on, answering the shots from *Indefatigable*'s weary powder-blackened gunners; the intermittent reports, punctuating the continuous *clank-clank-clank* of the pumps, were scarcely audible above the din of shrieking wind and roaring sea. Four bells of the morning watch, but no slightest sign of dawn. A sudden rift blew in the clouds and hazy moonlight showed the ghastly waves rising like tall spectres, the plunging battleship careering through them. It showed more than that to George Bell, fourth lieutenant, whose station was on the forecastle. He fought his way aft shouting and gesturing frantically.

'Breakers ahead! Land—land dead ahead!'

From the quarterdeck they saw the line of white breakers as the frigate rose. The French coast; and a bare two miles away. Pellew's orders came instantly and were relayed along the spray-swept deck.

'All guns cease fire—hands to the braces—stand by to go about!'

To go about! The words echoed ominously in Jeremiah Coghlan's mind. He was no stranger to gales and rough seas (though such a storm as this was beyond his experience) and he knew that the thing was impossible. To bring her broadside-on to wave and gale in these enormous seas, as must be done before she could turn away from danger, must inevitably send her waterlogged hull to the bottom. With a hand grasping the lee mizzen brace and the other clutching the rail he waited tensely.

'Ready about!'

Pellew and Thomson were both down at the wheel with the quartermasters.

'Heave-o!—Well enough!'

Indefatigable's bow lurched slowly round as she sank into a black trough. For an instant she hesitated and it seemed that she would miss stays. Then, rising on a long slope of water, she caught the wind, her topsails filling with a thunderous clap. Far, far over she lay with the watery ballast in her holds dragging her down. Sluggishly, reluctantly, she came up, her deck emptying like a weir, and with a crash of plunging bows drew off on the larboard tack.

'Make fast, all!' came Pellew's shout. 'Mr Thomson, send a hand to the foremasthead.'

Jeremiah gulped with relief and told himself that never would he see a piece of seamanship to equal that. In the flying minutes of tension the fight with *Droits de l'Homme* had been thrust completely from his mind. It was in fact the excited voices from the quarterdeck that recalled his last sight of her—rushing blindly onward towards what must be her doom. The frigate hoisted herself on a crest and he saw the French 80-gun ship plainly in the moonlight.

On the long white surf-line, still too close astern, a dark hulk lay with great waves breaking over it. *Droits de l'Homme*, dismasted and driven ashore, was a total wreck. The news spread along the deck and *Indefatigable*'s men raised a shrill cheer. On the quarterdeck Midshipman FitzJames shook his fist ferociously.

'Drown 'em!' he yelled excitedly, presumably to the pounding seas. 'Drown 'em! Drown every damned Frog of 'em!'

Pellew turned on him fiercely. 'Belay that baby talk, boy,' he rasped. 'By the Lord, I'd send my boats to help them—and you, Mr FitzJames, in one of the boats—if I thought they'd stay afloat for half-a-minute in this sea. Mark this, sir. As long as he can fight back a Frenchman's an enemy to be killed. When his ship's gone he's a life to be saved.'

His voice came clearly above the clamour of wind and sea, and Jeremiah, at the rail below the quarterdeck, heard and admired and did not forget.

An instant afterwards a very different cry rose from the frigate's decks. Half-a-mile to the left of the wrecked Frenchman along the pale band of frothing shoals they saw *Amazon* driving helplessly into the flurry. They saw her strike, her masts going by the board; saw the seas boil round her hull and hide it. But after that there was nothing to be discerned of the fate of her crew. And the storm roared on, indifferent to the doom of hunter and hunted.

Captain Pellew could do nothing for his wrecked consort. The fate of his own ship still hung in the balance, and within the hour her chances of survival were drastically reduced. Talley the master had surmised that the land ahead was the coast of Ushant, and if that was so *Indefatigable* had open sea before her. But as the dingy grey light of dawn spread over the waste of leaping waves there came a shrill hail from the masthead that set the captain racing up to the foretop to see for himself. Stretching right across the frigate's course, black uneven teeth jetting white water on the horizon, was a line of reefs. This was not Ushant. This was Audierne Bay far to the south, and *Indefatigable* was embayed on a lee shore. If she was not to suffer the fate of the other two ships she must fight for her life.

For four mortal hours the frigate's worn-out crew toiled at the ropes and the pumps, tacking every few minutes, clawing desperately off the seemingly endless rank of reefs. Men sank to the deck and slept where they lay when, a little before noon, all danger was past and the open sea lay before them. In a gale that at last showed some sign of moderating the frigate shaped a course for England.

3

'I believe she'll bear another reef out, Mr Thomson,' said Pellew.

'Aye aye, sir,' said the first lieutenant doubtfully, and leant over the taffrail to shout the order.

Hand-over-hand the men dashed up the

weather shrouds, and with them went the midshipmen of the watch, glad enough to exercise their numbed bodies. The wind was still at gale force, but *Indefatigable* had made her landfall off the Lizard in the first light of January 15th and was on a course east-north-east with a quartering wind, so that her masts lay over less steeply than they had done. Those masts were in a state that justified the first lieutenant's doubt of the wisdom of making more sail. The guns of *Droits de l'Homme* had left them gashed and splintered in a score of places, and though boatswain and carpenter had contrived a fishing for the wounded mainmast and had rigged preventers on the badly-strained mizzen there would be no setting of all plain sail again until extensive refitting had been done.

It was a miracle that they had stood through that long struggle out of Audierne Bay. The frigate's rigging was in a bad way, too, despite long and difficult work by Hannay and his men. As he climbed to the mizzen top Midshipman Coghlan noted the multitude of splices in shrouds and running rigging and the white gash in the spanker boom below him.

Since yesterday's long hours of tension Jeremiah had been able to get a watch-below of deep unbroken sleep and fill his belly with beef and biscuit. He had also paid a visit to the sick-bay where Delamere lay with a splinter wound in his thigh. *Indefatigable* had nineteen wounded all told, and though two of these had suffered amputation and hovered between life and death no one had been killed outright. The realisation that he himself had come unscathed through successive perils, that life still held its smiling promise, made the dark morning seem bright and the angry Channel waves below his feet benevolent.

With the swaying topsail yard under his armpits and his feet on the footrope he shuffled out with the rest. His neighbour on the right, he saw, was Charles Paddon, who must have been first up the shrouds. First on the yard, last off it; he had better keep an eye on the lad when it came to the awkward business of regaining the shrouds. Paddon's thin face was drawn and blue with cold, tight mouth and staring eyes betraying the narrow mastery of his fear as his numbed fingers wrestled with the reef-knot. Jeremiah felt a roughness under the instep and glancing down saw that the footrope was frayed, one of the strands parted and another ready to go. Job for Mr Hannay there. He cast loose his knot. Along the yard the other hands were jumping for the shrouds. The sail bellied out with a bang and in the same instant the shouted orders from down on deck sounded above the ceaseless clank of the pumps.

'Sheet home . . . well . . . belay all.'

Jeremiah began the sideways shuffle along the

footrope. One step, and he was hanging from the yard by his arms and the parted rope was streaming out on the wind.

His legs swung inward under the curve of the topsail but with an elbow clamped over the round of the spar he could steady himself in some degree of balance despite the rocking of the yard. The mast and its shrouds were no more than ten feet to his left and he could swing himself along to the shrouds without much difficulty. He looked over his right shoulder. Paddon had evidently not begun to move inboard when the footrope failed, for he was a dozen feet away right out at the end of the yardarm.

The slant of the mizzen-mast, tilting the swaying yard, placed him well above Jeremiah, as if he was on the upper end of a see-saw, and he was dangling with one arm over the yard and trying to get hold with the other. As Jeremiah watched he succeeded in raising his weight on both elbows and hung with the gale thrusting at his legs.

'You're all right now, man!' Jeremiah shouted at him. 'Work your way down to me and I'll lend a hand!'

Paddon slowly turned his face, but he made no reply. The wind tore at his long black hair, streaming it out like a pennant.

'Shuffle your arms along. Lively, now, or your strength'll go.'

'It's gone. I—cannot.'

The boy's voice was steady enough but the note of utter despair was unmistakable. Jeremiah glanced at the green surge of waves directly beneath him. On the strip of deck that he could see men were moving about their duties; no one seemed to have seen what was happening aloft. He heaved his body sideways and got his left leg over the yard, heaved again and was sitting astride. With his heel bumping on the straining canvas of the sail he began to hitch himself up the slant of the yard, thrusting with both hands in front of his thighs. Paddon's head was down on his clinging arms. The pitch and whip of the mast seemed likely to dislodge him at any moment. When he was close to Paddon Jeremiah took firm hold with his left hand, swung the other leg over so that both lay against the taut curve of the sail, and got his right hand under the other's armpit.

'Right hand over here. Up with your right leg when I heave. *Now!*'

For an instant he thought Paddon would slip back, and next moment, when their combined effort brought him sprawled precariously on the yard, that both of them would go flying down the bulge of the topsail, but Paddon steadied himself astride and he was able to regain his position. They sat facing each other with a leg each side of the yard and their hands clutching it.

Jeremiah grinned. 'It's like the pillow-fight on a greased pole in Polruan cove—except we've no pillows.'

There was no answering grin from the boy. His white face was set, expressionless as a mask, as if all his will was devoted to showing no emotion. Jeremiah placed his big hands over Paddon's thin ones.

'I've got you safe,' he said. 'You'll come on as I make sternway. Hitch along when I give the word. Now . . . Now . . . Now.'

Inch by inch, balancing their bodies against the savage thrust of the wind, they progressed down the yard. Jeremiah glanced over his shoulder.

'Into the shrouds next—easy.' He could feel Paddon shaking violently. 'Hold tight and I'll get you across.'

He got his foot to the ratlines and hooked a hand firmly. Paddon half-fell across the gap and was pinned flat against the shrouds by Jeremiah's arm. He seemed on the point of collapse.

'I'm going down first,' Jeremiah said. 'Take hold with your hands and I'll look after your feet.'

Slow enough it was, with a pause at every step down the wet rope-rungs, but at last they came down through a drench of flying spray to the deck. As they stood at the rail, Jeremiah's hand still grasping Paddon's arm, Bolton the third lieutenant came hurrying past on his way to the quarterdeck.

'What's this? What's this?' he demanded, stopping. 'Lady's day on the mizzen-shrouds? A fit of swooning aloft?'

'Footrope parted, sir, mizzen topsail yard,' said Jeremiah smartly. 'Mr Paddon hurt his arm and I lent him a hand.'

'Oh,' said Bolton. 'Report that parted rope to the boatswain, Mr Coghlan. And get your quarters squared-up, d'ye hear? We'll be off Falmouth Bay in an hour.'

He passed on. Jeremiah was left facing Paddon. The boy had mastered his trembling but his face was still set and expressionless. He threw his head back and met Jeremiah's eyes.

'I believe you saved my life, Mr Coghlan,' he said evenly. 'Thank you.'

He turned away towards the after-hatch. Jeremiah scratched his head and trotted for'ard to seek Mr Hannay.

4

A great deal was made in England of the destruction of the *Droits de l'Homme* by two frigates, but not until some weeks had passed. A dilatory Government, shaking in its shoes, had been unable to prevent the news of the Irish invasion plan from spreading and Pitt's stock was almost as low as that of Admiral Lord Bridport in the minds of the public. Everyone knew that sheer laxness had allowed the French fleet and 15,000 troops to cross the seas to Ireland and that only the chance of unusually bad weather had stopped a French army from landing on the west coast of England. The comfortable barriers of the encircling sea and the invincible Royal Navy were suddenly seen to be penetrable after all.

To plug this leakage of confidence the authorities gave full rein to their encomiums of the long night chase by *Indefatigable* and *Amazon*. The credit of Captain Sir Edward Pellew rose as Lord Bridport's declined. Never, declared the *Morning Post*, had British courage, seamanship and fighting spirit been so emphatically displayed; and went on to spread itself into extra pages with the story of the action and the news, lately received, of Captain Reynolds and his men.

Amazon's entire ship's company, it appeared, had been saved. Every man including those who had been wounded were at present prisoners in the town of Plouarnec, where they were being kindly treated by the Breton townspeople. The moment she had struck Captain Reynolds had set his crew to the construction of rafts, and by means of these and the admirable discipline that prevailed every soul on board had come safely through the surf to dry land.

How different (exclaimed the *Post*) was the case of the *Droits de l'Homme*! And proceeded to quote in full the account sent by a certain Lieutenant Pipon, an English prisoner who had been on board. Though she had grounded only 200 yards from the beach, where upwards of 500 persons had collected, the Frenchman had lost more than 1,000 of her people by drowning or by violence on board. Panic and utter chaos among the men, the relinquishing of all responsibility by the officers, the substitution of *sauve qui peut* for ordered behaviour in the face of danger, had brought disaster on the heels of disaster. Nothing could show more plainly (ended the enthusiastic journalist) the weakness of vessels manned by Jacobin regicides when matched against the ships of our gallant navy.

This was a small sop to the Cerberus of public opinion, which growled increasingly against a Government that could leave a trio of frigates to cope with twenty-one ships of the line. But four weeks later there came news that superseded the nine days' wonder of Pellew's success. Sir John Jervis had won a great victory off Cape St Vincent, defeating the combined French and Spanish fleets and taking four enemy battleships. Admiralty could hold up its head again. Admiral Lord Bridport, his nearly fatal inactivity conveniently forgotten, could continue to exercise his powers.

Sir Edward Pellew's criticism of his senior

officer, both implied and open, had not been forgotten. Lord Bridport removed him from the independent command where he had caused so much nuisance and appointed him captain of *Impetueux*, 74. As for *Indefatigable*, long overdue for refit, she went into dock after paying off, and since Pellew was severely limited as to the number of officers he could take with him to his new command her company was dispersed.

Midshipman Jeremiah Coghlan found himself posted to one of the Portsmouth guard-ships, an ageing sloop commanded by an elderly and gin-soaked junior lieutenant. The fact that he was second in command was little compensation for the loss of his friends and his hero.

CHAPTER FIVE

THE DOG AND THE SNAKE

1

The little cemetery on the hill at Watton overlooked the valley of the Brit where the river twisted out into the sea by way of Bridport harbour. May sunshine glittered on the white flecked blue of the Channel beyond falling green slopes gold-powdered with buttercups.

Midshipman Jeremiah Coghlan, ducking beneath the black shadow of the lych-gate, experienced a sudden lifting of his spirits; a sombre period of his life was left behind him here, and the bright prospect ahead seemed to him an infallible warranty of future success. He was, after all, only twenty-five.

Abner Best closed the lych-gate behind them and put on his hat.

''Tis mighty convenient here for tending the grave,' he said, 'and Mary was Dorset born. Your father—' He checked himself and cleared his throat. 'He was a Cornishman, o'-course.'

The two went on down the grassy path, for a while in silence. It was the third time that Jeremiah had visited his mother's grave. He had not seen her again before she died—a death too long foreseen for any shock of surprise—and Captain Best had dealt with the burial and the disposal of the Polruan cottage before his news had reached her son at Portsmouth.

If Jeremiah felt sorrow at his loss it was all but banished by the resurgence of hope and ambition. Two burdens had fallen from his shoulders: a past of which he had come to be ashamed, and the unrewarding service of past months in the Portsmouth guard-ship. He fingered the crumpled letter in his pocket, a talisman that should set his feet once more on the ladder of fame. Dated May 15th, 1800, it requested and required Midshipman Coghlan to proceed forthwith on board His Majesty's frigate *Amethyst* at Plymouth for passage to the West Indies, where he would join the squadron commanded by Sir Edward Pellew, Commodore.

Abner paused on a corner of the steep path to sniff the morning breeze. 'Southerly and like to hold,' he pronounced. 'You'll be round Bolt Head afore first light tomorrow.—Yonder's Matt's lugger,' he added. 'We've time for a pint.'

From the hill-brow they could see right along the coast to westward, where a brown speck on the blue sea-plain a mile off Charnock moved slowly. Matt Shipton's small lugger had been engaged to take Jeremiah and his sea-chest round to Plymouth and set him on board *Amethyst*. They walked on down the zigzag lane under the scented hedges of pink and white wild-rose and came out between whitewashed cottages to Bridport harbour. Captain Best's brig *Colombe* lay alongside the quay with men busy about her embarking coils of hawser, and a cart laden with more coils was rumbling down the lane from the ropewalks of Bridport town a mile-and-a-half up river.

'How's it feel being within the law, Abner?' Jeremiah asked with a grin as they went through the inn door.

'Why, well enough,' replied the captain seriously. 'It's quiet-like, but the Lord don't spare us with years, lad. I'm a mite too old for the Trade, I reckon.—Two tankards o' the best ale, Will.'

They sat down by the window and Will brought their pints.

'Off to jine Sir Ed'ard Pellew, I hear,' he said to Jeremiah. 'A prime seaman as ever was, next to Lord Nelson. Guesting wi' Squire Hardy up in Bridport last October, was Sir Ed'ard.'

'Captain Pellew in Bridport?' said Jeremiah as the landlord went away. 'You didn't tell me, Abner.'

Captain Best buried his nose in his tankard and drank deep before he answered. 'Slipped my memory, I reckon. A deal o' things does that nowadays. Ay—it was before he sailed with the squadron for the Indies. And as to that, I'd as lief you was with Lord Nelson as with Cap'n Pellew. The French rascals took a walloping at the Nile, but they've a big fleet in Brest again. That's where you'd make a reppitation—the Biscay coast and the Mediterranean. These Sugar Isles is fussed over to please the City merchants. Now if Pitt—'

Jeremiah heard his exposition of high policy with small attention. He suspected Abner Best of being less than open with him. What business could have brought Edward Pellew to Bridport, that Abner was so loth to mention his visit?

'Well,' he said when the captain paused for a

drink, 'to the West Indies I go, so there's an end of that. As to why I go—I've been thinking of it. Captain Pellew was well disposed towards me, Abner, as you know. D'you think he might have asked for me to be sent out?'

Abner set down his tankard and wiped froth from his lips. 'Ah, there's no knowing,' he said, smoothing his beard with a judicial air. 'From what he said, now—'

He caught himself up quickly and seized Jeremiah's empty tankard.

'Will! Two more.—You'll be dry enough, likely, before Matt's off Berry Head. Best make the most o' your chance, lad. You won't get ale as good—'

'Belay, there!' Jeremiah broke in sharply. 'How come you to know what Captain Pellew said?'

''Twas a manner of speaking, lad,' mumbled the captain. 'Tongues wag in Bridport town, and a man gets to hear this and that.'

'You can't gammon me, Cap'n Best. Come now—you spoke with Captain Pellew yourself, Abner, didn't you?'

Abner tugged at his beard, looked left and right, perceived Will coming with the ale and welcomed him with unconvincing exuberance.

'Right good ale, Will—no better brew in England. I was telling Mr Coghlan here, he'll taste nothing like this down Jamaica way.'

'Reckon 'tis rum he'll drink thereaways,' said

Will, departing, 'and none o' your watered grog neither.'

Jeremiah sipped at his tankard without taking his eyes from his companion's face, or what could be seen of it behind the big pewter mug.

'So you had some talk with Captain Pellew, Abner,' he said, restraining a grin at the captain's embarrassment. 'Maybe it was confidential. Or maybe there was some mention of me you can pass on without forswearing yourself. Did he call on you?'

Abner slowly lowered the tankard, tugged his beard again, and nodded. 'All right, lad. Sir Ed'ard did me the honour to call at my house, d'ye see. Being as he was staying at Squire Hardy's place, and wishful—so he said—to shake the hand o' *Colombe*'s master. That little matter o' the *Upnor Castle* four years ago, he was thinking of. By a providence I'd a bottle of the cognac handy and we took a dram together. Aye—we drank to your good fortune, Jeremiah, Sir Ed'ard proposing.'

'So there was talk of me?'

'In a manner. Sir Ed'ard was asking about your—your family, and schooling, and that. Right sorry he was to hear o' your ma's passing-on.'

'But about the West Indies station?'

Abner passed a hand across his brow. 'I'll tell you plain what he said, lad, and then you can stop your pestering. A Portsmouth guard-boat's no place for a promising young officer like Mr Coghlan, says Sir Ed'ard. I'll find him something better afore a twelvemonth's gone, he says. So there's for you.'

Jeremiah's smile of pleasure changed to a frown.

'I don't see why you kept this to yourself,' he said. 'There's no harm in my knowing.'

'It was Sir Ed'ard's desire,' began Abner, and stopped to take a long drink of ale.

For some seconds the eyes visible on either side of his tankard's rim shifted their gaze nervously as if in search of inspiration. Possibly the best brew in England bestowed it on him, for he set the mug down with a thump and stared earnestly at the tall midshipman.

'I'll tell you why, Jeremiah Coghlan,' he said hurriedly. 'It's that I don't want to see you get uppish. You've interest with Sir Ed'ard—well enough. Don't presume on it, lad. Pride goeth before destruction and an haughty spirit before a fall, which is the word o' your namesake the prophet and the word o' the Lord, d'ye see. Likewise, put not thy trust—'

'Here's Matt tying up alongside,' called Will from the doorway.

Captain Best jumped to his feet with alacrity.

'And little enough tide left to serve,' he said briskly, going to the door. 'Matt ahoy! Belay that—he's coming aboard at the jump.'

The peak of the brown sail that appeared at

the quay's edge reascended to the block. Jeremiah picked up his sea-chest and followed his foster-father across the stones to the little lugger. Red-bearded Matt Shipton stowed the chest in the sternsheets, nodded at his passenger, and jerked a thumb towards the jib sheets. A mighty grip from Abner's oak-hard hand and a mumbled blessing, and then Matt shoved off. Between them they tacked her neatly out through the narrow harbour entrance into the sparkling chop of the Channel, with a last glimpse of Captain Best's stocky figure on the quay before the harbour wall hid him from sight.

'Haul in a mite, mister,' said Matt, speaking for the first time.

Jeremiah took in a foot of jib sheet and secured it with a half-hitch on the cleat. As the lugger sped westward with a soldier's wind over her beam he reflected, frowning, on Abner's odd behaviour. At the last, the captain had seemed anxious to be rid of him. And was he, Jeremiah, justly to be called uppish? Ambition such as he owned wasn't uppishness; any midshipman in the Service must aspire to be rated lieutenant, to achieve post-captain and even admiral. As to pride, there was no sin in a man's being proud of his seamanship or his ship. Knowing Abner as he did, Jeremiah was acquainted with the captain's tendency to scriptural quotation when he had something to hide, and he had more than a suspicion that he had not been told all that had taken place at Abner's meeting with Captain Pellew.

But here was the Wear Cliff gleaming white beyond the blue waves to starboard, and this was the beginning of that long westward voyage—six weeks, five perhaps if the wind was fair—that would end in the Caribbean. And one thing was certain from Abner's flummery: he had not lost interest with Captain Pellew, Jeremiah had learned that he would be the most junior of the dozen or so officers, some of them military, that were being sent to the West Indies station. He felt reasonably sure, now, that Sir Edward had himself requested the services of Mr Midshipman Coghlan, and the bright morning shone the brighter for it.

2

Under a cloudless sky, across waters of a darker blue than those off Bridport harbour, *Amethyst*'s boat pulled towards the flag-ship. Jeremiah Coghlan, in the sternsheets beside the silent Captain Digby, turned his rapturous gaze from the big ships ahead to the land two miles away to starboard. The high green mountains of Martinique hung there against the sky (one of the more distant peaks was plumed with smoke) and below them at sea-level were the white buildings of Fort-de-France, the principal French naval base in the West Indies.

He could see the spars of the line-of-battle ship and three frigates that lay in the harbour, the big grey walls of the forts that defended it, and the three gun-brigs that were moored outside covering the entrance. Those forts mounted 250 guns in all, Captain Digby had told him. The two battleships of Sir Edward Pellew's squadron could have no hope of successful attack on such a fortress; they could only blockade the naval base, preventing reinforcement and holding the French warships immobilised.

His attention returned to the big 74 they were fast approaching. *Impetueux* had backed her topsails, as had the three ships beyond her, and lay almost motionless with her great brown hull with its double row of chequered gunports reflected in the glassy water. Beyond her an armed cutter glided slowly under reefed mainsail and jib; *Amethyst* had come out to supplement this, the squadron's one scout and messenger.

'Quicken stroke,' snapped Digby, a man of few words.

Jeremiah had had time, during the long voyage out from England, to learn to appreciate Captain Digby's rigid discipline and stern efficiency. He had some reason, too, to think that the captain appreciated his own capabilities. *Amethyst* was short-handed on the quarterdeck, her third lieutenant having died of a fever on the fifth day out from Plymouth, and Midshipman Coghlan had been called upon to perform the duties of fourth lieutenant.

Then, after the frigate had put her soldier-officer passengers ashore at Kingston, there had been the capture off Santo Domingo, with only two shots fired, of a Spanish merchantman, requiring another of *Amethyst*'s lieutenants to be detached to take the prize back into Kingston; so that for the better part of a week Jeremiah had been in effect third lieutenant. He knew that he had done well in these positions, though Digby was not given to praise.

The boat came smartly alongside below the entry port, the narrow black shadow under *Impetueux*'s side bringing welcome coolness after the blaze on the open water. The shrilling of boatswain's pipes sounded as the frigate's captain climbed on board, with Jeremiah following after a decent interval; the white-gloved sideboys, the red-coated marines presenting muskets, were not there for a mere midshipman's participation. The marines were dismissing and the ceremonial groups breaking up when he arrived on deck and touched his hat to the quarterdeck.

Any idea of his own importance that might have been in Midshipman Coghlan's mind quickly vanished. No one had any interest in him. Sir Edward Pellew's well-remembered form was up there above the taffrail exchanging salutes and handshakes with Captain Digby, after which the two officers came down the ladder and went into the stern cabin without a glance in his direction. He stood by the rail, glanced at incuriously by occasional deckhands passing about their duties, ignored by the officer of the watch and a lieutenant of marines who were chatting animatedly together on the other side of the after-deck.

He was a little overawed by the spaciousness and spruceness of this wide after-deck. The planking had been holystoned and scrubbed to immaculacy, the cordage at the entry port was dazzling in its whiteness. The halyards at the mainmast-foot were flemished down in coils of geometrical perfection, the brasswork of binnacle and wheel sparkled blindingly in the sun, and the two quartermasters at the helm were dressed in spotless white and wore ribbons on their straw hats. It was all as different as could be from the sluttish little guard-ship at Portsmouth. For five minutes or more he stood looking about him and wondering whether he ought to tell the coxswain in the boat below to send up his sea-chest.

A slight bustle by the larboard rail attracted his attention and a signal hoist rose smoothly to *Impetueux*'s yardarm. Jeremiah had learned his duties as signal-midshipman aboard *Indefatigable* and read the coloured bunting without difficulty: *numeral 5, close flagship, send boat*. The numeral flag was the armed cutter's number, for he could see her tall mast and the upper part of her big mainsail moving nearer beyond the opposite rail. Then a junior lieutenant of about his own age bustled up to him.

'Mr Coghlan? Please to follow me.'

He walked quickly to the entry of the stern cabin with Jeremiah at his heels. The marine sentry clicked to attention as they went in; the lieutenant said, 'Mr Midshipman Coghlan, sir,' and retreated.

The Commodore was standing with Captain Digby by the big stern windows of a spacious room whose white-painted deck-head reflected the dancing light from the waves and showed Edward Pellew little changed from three years ago; perhaps a little greyer, the lean brown face perhaps a little harsher in expression, but erect and instinct as ever with command. The frigate captain stepped back to bow stiffly and left the cabin with a curt nod for Jeremiah as he passed.

'Well, Mr Coghlan,' said Pellew.

Jeremiah advanced and stood with his hat under his arm. The Commodore's narrowed brown eyes surveyed him for a moment.

'I've a good report of you from Captain Digby,' he said without further preamble. 'It confirms an intention I had already formed. You—um—gained some experience of command at Portsmouth, I believe?'

Jeremiah remembered the drunken lieutenant and the many times he had perforce surrendered responsibility to his midshipman. 'On occasion, sir,' he said.

'Yes,' said Pellew. 'Lieutenant Pengelly, until recently commanding the cutter *Viper*—you saw her, doubtless, as you came on board—has been made second into *Pegasus*. You will take command of *Viper*. I shall rate you acting lieutenant, Mr Coghlan, which as you're aware betokens the possibility of a lieutenant's commission should you prove worthy of it.'

'Th—thank you, sir,' Jeremiah stammered. 'I shall try—'

'Attend, if you please. Normally a fourteen-gun cutter would have two lieutenants on the quarterdeck. In your case the second-in-command will have to be a midshipman. You'll have boatswain, carpenter, cook—'

Jeremiah, dazzled and somewhat dazed by this sudden bright flowering of his future, had some ado to comprehend the Commodore's rapid recital of *Viper*'s particulars. He managed to understand that she carried six 4-pounders, four 6-pounders, and eight swivels, that her crew numbered forty-six hands in a fair state of training which he was expected to improve, and that her chief duties would be inshore observation of the enemy and communication between the ships of the squadron.

'*Viper*'s boat will be alongside now,' said Sir Edward. 'You'll take over your command at once.' He paused. 'You will find a couple of past acquaintances on board the cutter. Camden, boatswain's mate in *Indefatigable*, is rated boatswain in her. Your second-in-command is Charles Paddon.'

His eyes were fixed intently on the midshipman's face as he spoke the last sentence and Jeremiah's start of dismay, though it was instantly controlled, did not escape him. A curious little smile curled the Commodore's lips. He held out his hand.

'Good luck to you, Mr Coghlan.'

'Thank you, sir,' said Jeremiah again.

He was out in the blinding sunlight without realising how he got there and hardly noticed the same junior lieutenant escorting him to the entry port. *Amethyst*'s boat had gone, and the smaller boat that had taken its place at the foot of the ladder had something that looked like a shining pink egg in the stern-sheets. Camden's bald pate was replaced by Camden's broken-toothed grin as he looked up.

'Right good to see ye again, sir,' he said as Jeremiah stepped down to the thwart.

Then they were pulling round the cliff-like

stern of *Impetueux* and across the sparkling water to the cutter. Jeremiah had eyes only for his new command. She was hove-to with her huge mainsail brailed-up and jib fluttering, the single mast twice as tall as the length at waterline of her low hull, which was pierced at the rail for six guns on the starboard side that was towards him. For an instant he was back on board *Colombe* watching the approach of the smart Navy cutter from the convoy; his hopeless ambition of nearly four years ago was now to be fulfilled after all. But there was a very large fly in this unctuous jar of ointment. Charles Paddon was to be his second-in-command.

Jeremiah well understood that as the sloop's commanding officer, with the right to be styled 'captain' on all occasions, it was his duty to hold himself above and aloof from his 'foremast hands. He and Paddon were the only quarterdeck officers in this tiny craft, Paddon was the only person with whom he could converse or confer. They two would have to live together at very close quarters with the absolute minimum of privacy and no chance of avoiding each other's company for days and weeks, perhaps months or even years.

Yet during the four months of Jeremiah's service in *Indefatigable* Paddon had steadily shown himself averse to any friendly communication between them. How was he to promote efficiency and maintain discipline, how justify his appointment, when such a state of things obtained? If Sir Edward knew of Paddon's attitude—and surely he did—he must also know that the situation was impossible.

'Boat ahoy!' came the hail from the cutter's deck. 'What boat's that?'

The patently unnecessary challenge meant that someone on board intended to preserve correct procedure.

'*Viper!*' Camden roared in reply, thereby indicating that the cutter's captain was in the boat.

They sheered neatly alongside and Jeremiah threw a leg over the rail. *Viper* was very nearly flush-decked, having only a foot rise abaft the after-hatch, but he saluted a visionary quarterdeck as he stepped on board. An evident attempt at ceremonial confronted him. Eight seamen stood formed in two lines, four a side (the cutter's narrow deck would hardly allow more) and at the opposite end of this avenue stood Midshipman Paddon arrayed in the whitest of breeches and wearing a silver-hilted dirk.

'Welcome aboard, sir,' said Paddon woodenly, doffing his hat. 'Pray excuse me.' He addressed his reception party. 'Hands to secure sea-boat! Hoist the command pendant, Finney! For'ard there—off brailings and haul taut.'

He had changed since Jeremiah had last seen

him; the slim figure had broadened out, the thin handsome face was red-brown instead of pale—but expressionless as of old when he faced the acting-lieutenant.

'The squadron's making sail, sir. Our station's half-a-league on the flagship's beam.'

'Thank you, Mr Paddon.'

Jeremiah threw one quick glance amidships where the boat was being swung inboard, another aloft, and a third at the helmsman standing by the long tiller. He made his orders ring sharp and clear.

'Main and jib sheets. Helm a-starboard, quartermaster. Meet her—steady as you go. Belay, all.'

The cutter heeled and curtseyed to the light breeze and skimmed away like a bird with the slow-moving squadron on her starboard quarter. Acting-lieutenant and midshipman stood balancing to the motion, not looking at each other, while she crossed the blue water to take up station.

'Helm a-lee,' said Jeremiah with an eye on *Impetueux* away on the starboard beam. 'Steady.'

'May I show you your quarters, sir?' said Paddon.

'Certainly,' Jeremiah turned to the boatswain, who had come trotting aft. 'Take the deck, Mr Camden, if you please. See that you keep her on station.'

'Aye aye, sir,' said Camden, settling himself comfortably astride by the helm.

The tiny after-cabin into which Paddon led the way was lit only by the opening of the hatchway and gloomy after the brilliance on deck. Bench-lockers, a table, a narrow door in either bulkhead leading to cramped sleeping quarters, were discernible. With headroom of less than five feet it was not easy to stand in any posture, and Jeremiah sat down on a locker. Paddon remained standing, as erect as the low deckhead allowed.

'Mr Coghlan,' he said, bringing the words out as if he willed them from his lips, 'I wish to make formal apology for my behaviour on board *Indefatigable*. I'm aware now that I gave cause for just resentment. I must plead that I was then younger, and have since learned—'

'For God's sake sit down, man!' said Jeremiah in a gust of relaxed tension.

'If you choose to resent it,' Paddon persisted doggedly, 'I am prepared to give you the satisfaction usual between gentlemen.' He sounded as if he had rehearsed his speech. 'However, in the interests of the present service I repeat that I—that I ask you to accept—'

'You'll obey my order and sit down.' Jeremiah barked the words; he was inclined to burst out laughing, though with relief rather than amusement. 'That's better. Now listen here, Paddon. I accept your apology, if that's what you want. You may believe I understood your feelings, though I didn't like the way you expressed 'em. But let bygones go. I'm captain here and you're my second. We'll make naught of *Viper* by nursing old grudges, so we'll—' He came to a stop. 'I've not your gift of the gab,' he ended with an embarrassed grin, 'but here's my hand on it.'

The midshipman hesitated before accepting the proffered hand but his brief grip was firm. They sat facing each other across the cabin table.

'Now, then,' said Jeremiah briskly. 'I'm the new boy here and I've a lot to learn. First, how long have you been second in *Viper*, Mr Paddon?'

'Five months. Since I was made midshipman—sir.'

So great was Jeremiah's relief at what had just passed that he was half minded to tell Paddon that his reluctant 'sir' could be omitted in the privacy of the cabin, but he quickly decided against it. Matters were not at that stage between them.

'I must rely a good deal upon you,' he said. 'Muster book and log can wait till tonight but there's other matters. You'll understand I've been appointed here at short notice—as short notice as ever a man was given, I reckon. Without your help I'm dismasted and sunk, Mr Paddon. I hope I can depend upon you to give it.'

This was simple truth; but had he sought to penetrate his companion's armour of pride he could not have found a better weapon.

'Of course, sir,' said Paddon with more warmth than he had yet shown.

'Very well, then. At this moment Camden's in charge of the deck, on my order. Is this in accordance with your usual practice?'

'Why, yes, sir. Camden's all right. Sober, good seaman—an old man-o'-war's man. Mr Pengelly used him as third officer and gave him a watch. We've got to have three watch-keepers and there's no one else.'

'So I surmised. Good set of hands?'

'Fairish. Smart enough at sheets and halyards but slow at the guns. Mr Pengelly ordered gun-drill once a week. In my opinion—'

'That's what I want,' said Jeremiah as he hesitated.

'I think there should be daily gun-drill, sir.'

'I agree. We'll see to it. What about our cook?'

'I suppose he might conceivably be worse.' Paddon was definitely unbending. 'The best thing he does is the duff on Wednesdays.'

'Come, that's not so bad,' said Jeremiah. 'Duff's a favourite with me. Any objection to duff every day, Mr Paddon?'

His eyes were accustomed now to the half-light in the cabin and he could not be mistaken: Charles Paddon was smiling. So far as he could recall it was the first time he had ever seen him smile.

'Not the least in the world, sir,' he said. 'And if there happened to be a sauce of rum and lime—'

'We'll see to that too. Now—I reckon an acting-lieutenant wouldn't pipe all hands and make a speech, so I'll go round the ship instead.' Jeremiah, getting to his feet, remembered in time to remain bent double. 'I'll thank you to act as guide, Mr Paddon. Forecastle, galley, store-room, powder-room—I want to see 'em all.'

'Aye aye, sir,' said Paddon cheerfully.

This was the beginning of what Jeremiah afterwards remembered as a halcyon period of his sea-life. By the end of that first day all restraint between himself and Charles Paddon had vanished, the last of it wiped away by their mutual determination to make *Viper* the finest warship of her class. When the sudden Caribbean night fell, Camden having the first watch, Paddon produced a bottle of passable claret bequeathed by her late captain and they drank together to the cutter's success and early promotion.

But the ordered calm of sunlit days at sea could not for long satisfy two ambitious officers one of whom was twenty-five and the other twenty. *Viper*'s occasional swift raids close inshore to observe what was going on in the harbour of Fort de France were their chief excitement and these soon palled. There was nothing going on in the harbour of Fort de France, or for that matter outside it.

Martinique, the main French base in the West Indies, was totally impregnable to assault from the sea. With the east coast of its 45-mile length shoal and dangerous and every practicable landing-place on the west defended by strong batteries the island offered no foothold for the most daring invasion attempt. The splendid harbour of Fort de France could not be bombarded by Pellew's ships without the risk of total annihilation of his squadron; the broadsides of *Impetueux* and *Pegasus* and *Hercule* were worse than useless against 250 big guns mounted in shore emplacements to cover harbour and bay. On the other hand the French 74 and the three frigates in Fort de France could make no move. It was stalemate.

So week after week the British squadron moved slowly to and fro, cruising between Diamond Point and the northern tip of Martinique, while the frigate *Amethyst* ranged the sea approaches beyond the horizon. As often as the patrolling ships brought the Castries headland on the bow the signal would flutter up to the flagship's yardarm and *Viper* would dash away on her flying inspection of the harbour. There was little enough for her to see and nothing of importance to report. Possibly the French defenders were well aware of this, or perhaps they disdained so insignificant a target, for the fortress guns did not fire on her though she was well within their range.

Midshipman Paddon was invariably incensed by this demonstration of contempt and Acting-Lieutenant Coghlan was scarcely less indignant. Still more annoying was the behaviour of the gun-brigs, particularly of the gun-brig *Cerbère*.

To frustrate any attempt by the British to penetrate the harbour with their boats by night the French had moored three gun-brigs across the entrance, two-masted vessels whose fighting strength was in their long 24-pounder guns. Their constant watchfulness was supplemented after nightfall by a guard-boat with a carronade mounted in the bows which pulled ceaselessly to and fro all night. When *Viper* paid her impudent visits of reconnaissance it might have been expected that the outermost gun-brig would try a shot or two at her, particularly as the cutter did not scruple to come within range of those 24-pounders; but instead the *Cerbère*'s crew, presumably instigated by their officers, indulged themselves with insult. The Union flag jiggled at a yardarm and hauled down with a rush, a screeched *Ça Ira* chorus audible across the water, and much ruder manual gestures clearly to be discerned through Jeremiah's glass—these were their substitutes for gunnery.

In all probability they were forbidden to fire unless fired upon, which were precisely *Viper*'s orders. The cutter's crew chafed under their captain's strict command that no reply in kind was to be made to this offensive *badinage*. Midshipman Paddon urged furiously that a cartel should be sent inviting *Cerbère* to come out and fight ship-to-ship; a plan that, delightful as it was, had no chance at all of the Commodore's approval. Acting-Lieutenant Coghlan, deciding that this was not to be borne, produced a scheme, complete in every detail, which he passed to his second-in-command for comment and approval.

That *Viper*'s officers knew a good deal about *Cerbère* was due to their taste for fresh fish, acquired when Seaman Connolly's duff had begun to pall. The dusky fishermen whose little craft plied the inshore waters of Martinique's west coast seemed perfectly indifferent to Anglo-French hostilities, and from them the cutter had often bought fish and acquired bits of information. They had learned *Cerbère*'s name, that she was newly-built and well-found, and that she carried between eighty and ninety men. She was plainly a worthy prize, and a night cutting-out expedition (said Jeremiah now) was the way to take her.

'Damned good!' crowed Paddon, wild with enthusiasm. 'But we've to get the Commodore's permission, Jerry.'

In the privacy of the cabin they were at Christian names now though on deck the 'sir' and 'mister' were never omitted.

'He'll have to give it,' said Jeremiah. 'We want his ten-oared cutter.'

He went on with his exposition. The present circumstances were propitious. In two days the squadron would be off Fort de France, there was no moon, and the cloud that had formed every night this past week would obscure the stars. *Amethyst* was with them on one of her periodical returns to the squadron and she could supply one boat; *Viper*'s sea-boat would do for the other. Three boats were needed, to board the gun-brig in succession at three separate points having approached unobserved. With the ten-oared cutter carrying a dozen men in addition to the oarsmen and another dozen in the two smaller boats they should have enough for the job.

'Any suggestions, Charles?' he finished.

'Well—you and I go, naturally. Camden can stay with *Viper*.'

Jeremiah hesitated for a moment. A cutting-out party could be a bloody business if things went wrong. He was assailed again by the curious feeling that he was in some way responsible for Charles Paddon, that he should hold him back from danger when possible. It was absurd. It was as much Charles's duty to take the risks of war as it was his own.

'That's of course,' he said.

A letter beginning 'I respectfully beg to submit' was delivered to *Impetueux* without delay, and without delay Mr Coghlan was summoned on board. Somewhat to his surprise the detailed plan Jeremiah had enclosed with his letter was approved by the Commodore, who stipulated only that twelve volunteers from *Impetueux* should be included in the party for the ten-oared cutter. Probably, he reflected, Sir Edward was as discontented at the continued lack of action as he was himself. In this he was not far wrong.

'If this enterprise succeeds, Mr Coghlan, you will have done a service to the squadron as well as for your country,' said Pellew, dismissing him. 'But—mark this—it must succeed.'

'Aye aye, sir,' said Mr Coghlan.

3

'Cerberus,' muttered Paddon, his lips close to Jeremiah's ear. 'He's the dog that guards the gate of Hades, you know.'

'Well, a dog's perished of snake-bite before now,' returned *Viper*'s captain in the same tone.

The two were squeezed close together in the sternsheets of the flagship's ten-oared cutter, Jeremiah's arm on the tiller and a seaman nursing a naked cutlass on either hand. Five oarsmen a side, the cutter sped swiftly across black water hardly rippled by the slight land-breeze, under a night sky so dark that it was only just possible to make out the uneven silhouette of the land ahead. One or two scattered lights showed ashore but there would be few folk wakeful in Fort de France at this hour of two in the morning.

'Do you see anything of the others?' asked Jeremiah, his gaze on the dim outline of the wooded peak he was using as a mark.

Paddon twisted round to look astern. 'Not a sight or a sound,' he answered after a pause.

It was according to plan that the boats from *Amethyst* and *Viper* should keep well astern of the cutter so as to attack in succession, but even with the land-breeze blowing towards them the faint sounds of their progress should have been audible. Jeremiah peered at the sugarloaf shape of the hill slowly growing up the slightly paler darkness of the sky above him; less than half-a-mile to pull now. He spoke in a low voice.

'Bows. Keep a lookout. Eyes skinned for the guard-boat.'

A man stood up from among the half-dozen seamen crouching in the bows.

'Dead silent, all,' said Jeremiah.

The rhythmic faint plash of the blades as they dipped, the rustle and creak of the looms in the cloth-muffled rowlocks, were the only sounds except the low hiss of water at the cutter's forefoot. A warm breath came from the land, a compound scent of spice and vegetation mingled with the taint of human ordure. The wooded peak rose higher, eyes long accustomed to the velvety darkness could discern the shapes of harbour buildings below it and then the fret of masts and spars. Jeremiah had just picked out the twin masts and hull of the outermost gun-brig when his eye caught the frantic gesturing of the man in the bows, an arm jabbing urgently to starboard. The guard-boat—but was it heading towards them or away? He edged the cutter's bows away to larboard, straining his eyes and ears in the dark, and made out the low black shape motionless a pistol-shot away in the same instant that a voice challenged loudly in French.

Those French seamen must have been resting on their oars. Run from them? The carronade could blast them out of the water. No hope of avoiding an alarm now.

'Pull!' he snapped. 'Pull for your lives!' and turned the cutter's bows straight for the guard-boat.

The cutter leaped forward like a spurred horse. Twenty fathoms of water to cover, and if they had that carronade ready and pointed—

'Boat oars, starboard! Cutlasses—board!'

He had intended to sheer alongside but

misjudged the distance in the darkness. The cutter's stem smashed into the guard-boat's side abaft the bows with a grinding shock that almost flung him from the helm and pitched Paddon on top of the men squatting below the stern thwart. Shouts, the thud of blows, a squeal of pain, and then a sudden yell of 'Shove off, quick!' The cutter moved astern amid a chorus of frightened voices from the guard-boat. Jeremiah saw the black shape of the other boat change, heard the chorus abruptly stilled as she rolled over and sank in a surge of phosphorescence.

'Foundered, by God!' gasped Paddon, struggling up. 'That carronade put her down—'

'Oars!' Jeremiah shouted, pushing the tiller hard over. 'Give way together, for all you're worth!'

'Double-bank 'er, sir?' suggested Furze, *Viper*'s big leading hand, from down by his knees.

'No time for that. Drive her, lads!'

Cerbère was less than a cable's length away, her big hull rapidly growing on the darkness. A light glinted and dodged along her deck and voices rang sharply. No hope now of surprise after the noisy skirmish with the guard-boat. Jeremiah spared only a passing thought for the loss of that counted-on advantage and the now doubtful support of the following boats, for his mind was fixed on the necessity for immediate attack. The cutter foamed through the water under the thrust of twenty powerful arms and the gun-brig's side reared close ahead.

'Stand by to board soon as we touch!'

A pistol flashed and banged right above him as he sheered the cutter alongside under *Cerbère*'s larboard bow, and in a moment he had grabbed his cutlass and was clawing for hold on her wooden side. Dark figures climbed beside him, others swarmed yelling overhead at the rail. Paddon's high-pitched cry cut through the din.

'Nets! 'Ware nets!'

Jeremiah had already encountered the gun-brig's boarding-netting. He was entangled by arm and leg in the sagging ropes, but his sword-arm was free and he slashed furiously, while someone—was it Charles?—climbed up past him and was thrust down again into the boat. A blinding flash a yard from his nose and an instant searing pain across his cheek was followed the next second by an agonising stab in his thigh as a boarding-pike jabbed savagely down at him. He swung his cutlass at the netting with all his strength. It gave way suddenly and he fell to land in a heap in the sternsheets. He struggled to his feet. Men were being tumbled back into the cutter and she was beginning to drift clear. He yelled to them to hook on. Shots and flashes came from the brig's rail and one of the seamen collapsed with a groan. He found Paddon beside him.

'Charles—all right?'

'All right,' panted the midshipman.

'Come on, then. Up, lads, and give a cheer!'

A hoarse shout, a screech from *Cerbère*'s men, and they were scrambling together up the Frenchman's side again. Jeremiah dashed aside the dangling net, warded off a swordstroke that jarred his lifted blade, and got a leg over the rail.

He had time for a backhanded sweep with the cutlass and a downstroke that cut flesh and bone before he was jammed against the rail by a press of yelling Frenchmen. His right hand was pinned to his side but he hit out with his left, a blind blow that failed to land and ended with his arm caught and held.

He heard Paddon shouting 'Damn you—*damn* you!' and an answering French oath an instant before he was pitched bodily outboard across the rail and into the boat, landing on his feet with a shock that brought excruciating pain to his wounded thigh. There was a second painful shock as Paddon came hurtling down upon him with a yell.

'Hurt, Charles?'

'Pinked in the shoulder.' Paddon was choking with rage. 'The bastard spat in my face. By God I'll—'

Jeremiah caught his arm as he was about to jump for the gun-brig's side. 'I'm going to draw off. Man the oars.'

'But damn it—'

'Obey my order.'

There was a heavy splash, and another, as two of the attacking seamen were flung over the rail into the water. Others were swarming down the side into the cutter, pursued by an uproar of shouts and jeers.

'Vipers!' Jeremiah bellowed. 'In the boat!'

A big man dropped like an ape from the foremast deadeyes. 'All away, sir,' panted Furze. ''Cept Mackay and 'e's copped it.'

'Give way!'

A pistol or two banged from the gun-brig's rail as the cutter turned from her, and splinters flew from the tiller close to Jeremiah's hand. The two men who had been flung overboard were hauled into the boat, bleeding from minor swordcuts but otherwise unhurt, and they made a hundred yards straight out into the darkness before resting on their oars while Jeremiah made a quick muster.

Mackay was absent, dead, according to Furze. Of the rest a number had wounds but only Cockerill, with a bullet in his knee, was incapacitated. He had twenty men to pit against four times that number. *But—mark this—it must succeed*. Where in God's name were the other boats? The French might be reinforced from their consorts any time now and if they were the chance was gone. Moreover, he could feel the hot blood still welling, soaking his breeches.

'Third time pays all, lads,' he said cheerfully. 'We'll have at 'em again. Are you with me?'

'Aye,' they growled. 'We'll show the buggers. We'll give 'em hell.'

'Give way, then, and smartly. Mr Paddon, in the bows. I shall board first over the quarter, you'll take your men into her over the bow. The word is Viper, men, and you'll not stop shouting it if you don't want your mates to cut you down.'

Swiftly they closed the gun-brig. An access of shouting told that the *Cerbère*'s men were ready for them. Jeremiah steered for her stern and sheer alongside under her quarter.

'Tiller, Cockerill.—Follow, Vipers!'

With a leap and a roar they were up, eight of them, stabbing and smiting with a fury that hurled back the French at the rail and gave them footing on the deck. For a few seconds it seemed that the violence of their onslaught would break the dense mob of their opponents. But though the dark mass of men gave back a pace or two they rallied with a yell and came on, pressing the British line back by sheer weight of numbers.

Jeremiah, sweeping left and right with his cutlass, could see little or nothing of individual opponents. A pistol flared a yard from his face, missing him, and he smashed his hilt into the jaw of the man who levelled it. Now his back was hard against the rail—and now came another roar, from for'ard along *Cerbère*'s deck.

'Viper! Viper!'

Paddon and his eleven men had boarded. Better than that—they had won ground, for the uproar of their fighting was somewhere near the foremast. Furze at Jeremiah's side burst a way forward bellowing like a bull.

'Ding 'em! Clout the sods!'

The crowd of Frenchmen swayed and broke. Jeremiah and the half-dozen with him battered their way for'ard along the deck, smiting with fist and cutlass. For perhaps thirty seconds their wild onslaught met with opposition. Then, with a suddenness that took them by surprise, the mass of their opponents seemed to melt away in the darkness. To left and right men were running across the deck to jump overside and swim for it, and before the two boarding-parties met amidships the deck was empty of Frenchmen except for the score of dark figures that lay writhing or motionless on the stained planking.

'Viper!' shouted Jeremiah hastily as someone came running at him.

Paddon gripped his arm. 'Done it!' he exulted breathlessly. 'And Jerry—the boats are here! They were closing us as we boarded.'

Jeremiah had lowered his cutlass-point to the deck and was leaning heavily on the hilt. He felt utterly spent, drained of the power to act or think. Yet quick thinking was vitally necessary now. Not a breath of wind here in the lee of the land. Useless to make sail.

'We'll tow her out.' It was an effort even to speak. 'Get for'ard, Mr Paddon. Use her halliards for towline—three of them. Make fast, one line to each boat, cut the bow mooring. A dozen men—into the cutter—the rest on board here.'

'Aye aye, sir.—You all right, Jerry?'

'Jump to it, damn you!'

Paddon dashed away for'ard, shouting. Jeremiah sucked in his breath and limped aft using the cutlass as a staff. The cable of the stern mooring was no more than five-inch hemp but it took an unconscionable time for his cutlass-strokes to sever it. There was a foolish satisfaction in cutting the lashing of the wheel with a single stroke, and immense relief when he could grasp the wheel-spokes and support himself against it. No sign of action from either of the other gun-brigs—likely enough their crews were ashore. Half-a-mile astern lights moved near the harbour entrance, and he could hear faint shouting. But a louder shout from *Cerbère*'s bows preceded a hardly perceptible jerk on her hull, then a more forcible tug, and now her bows began to swing. She was under way.

There was no room in his reeling thoughts for triumph, though he was vaguely conscious of small things; the moaning of a wounded Frenchman invisible somewhere by the mainmast, the fact that his own wound was still bleeding and that his right shoe was full of blood. He concentrated all his fast-waning strength on keeping the gun-brig from yawing and losing speed. Dimly at the back of his mind he knew that there was still danger to come.

How long it was before it came he did not know, for time had lost its meaning. The deep bellow of a gun from Fort de France woke him from a daze and he peered aimlessly for the fall of shot. There was another gun. And another. And then, silence, and darkness everywhere.

4

'I cannot refrain, my Lord, from expressing my admiration of that courage which, hand to hand, gave victory to a handful of brave fellows over four times their number, and of that skill which formed, conducted, and effected so daring an enterprise.'

So wrote Captain Sir Edward Pellew in his report to the First Lord, Earl St Vincent. It was a just comment. And yet, as Jeremiah admitted to himself, the daring enterprise would have been less desperate had he allowed for the faster speed of the ten-oared cutter, which had far outdistanced the other two boats in the black darkness.

No word of censure from the Commodore on this point reached Jeremiah, however; and indeed the acting-lieutenant was beyond censure or praise for many days, lying in a semi-conscious state in the sick-bay on board *Impetueux*. Excessive loss of blood and the ugly wound in his thigh induced a fever which caused Tierney the surgeon, deprived of his customary remedy of blood-letting, to shake his head dubiously, while the wound itself was grave enough to set him muttering about possible amputation. It was three weeks before Charles Paddon came below to the sick-bay to find his friend, pale and emaciated, sitting on the edge of his bunk with a stout stick handy.

'This is a sight for sore eyes, Jerry!' exclaimed Paddon delightedly as they exchanged hand-grips. 'How's the leg?'

'I can walk a step or two. Tierney says I'll always have a limp, though.' Jeremiah pointed to the strip of plaster crossing the midshipman's scalp. 'The Frogs just missed spoiling your beauty, Charles. They had a closer shot at mine.'

Paddon glanced at the livid three-inch scar that seamed Jeremiah's cheek between the eye and ear. 'It's an improvement,' he grinned. 'An honourable scar, and the girls'll love it. By the bye, did you know I was wounded in six places? All flesh-wounds, but it looks well in the report. They all healed to a miracle, Tierney says.'

'It's that blue blood of yours, young Charles.'

The look Paddon shot at him was sharp and questioning, but he smiled after a moment.

'Well,' he said, 'yours didn't do too badly, from what I hear. You've heard all the news, I suppose?'

'Some of it. I'd rather hear it from you. What about *Viper*'s wounded? Tierney said there were eight.'

'Eight there were, and they're all recovering. Mackay was killed you know—our only dead 'un. *Cerbère* had six killed and twenty wounded, far as we can make out.' Paddon's handsome face lit up and his dark eyes shone. 'D'you realise, Jerry, what a triumph it was? All due to you and everyone knows it. They'll know it in England too, when the Gazette gets hold of it. And as to the prize, *Cerbère*—well, what do you think?'

'Admiralty will buy her, perhaps?'

'That, of course. She's in first-rate trim. But it'll all come to you and me and the cutter's crew. The whole squadron would share normally but they've unanimously decided that it should go to the boat's crew that did the job.'

In all this there was immense satisfaction for Jeremiah, but it was his way to conceal emotion.

'Good of them,' he said. 'And what's the news of *Viper*?'

'Oh, Pengelly has her again, of course,' said

Paddon without enthusiasm. 'He's on board here now for orders. I came off in the boat with him, so I've not much time. The buzz is, Jerry—true or not I don't know—that when you're recovered you'll go to *Theseus* as fourth. That won't please me and the Vipers, I needn't tell you that.'

There was a patter of steps in the alleyway and a ship's boy stuck his head in at the door.

'*Viper*'s captain's on deck, sir!' he announced breathlessly.

'I must go.' Paddon went to the door and paused, looking back. 'Jerry,' he said hurriedly, 'I've written home. God knows when we'll be back in England but when we are there'll be shore leave and you'll come to stay with us at Trenythan. That's settled. Good luck to that leg!'

He was gone. Jeremiah lay back on the bunk and stared up at the low beams of the deckhead, seeing there rosy pictures of the future. Fame and fortune, perhaps, were still to seek, but he had achieved as much of both as any acting-lieutenant lacking influence or aristocratic connections could hope for. As *Viper*'s captain he would get the lion's share of the prize-money; if Charles was right about the appointment to *Theseus* it meant the practical certainty of a lieutenant's commission in the not-far-distant future. He would be sorry to lose *Viper*, but a full lieutenant in a ship of the line was a step up that quarterdeck ladder which he was resolved to climb to the topmost tread.

All this made the future very bright for Jeremiah Coghlan. But brightest of all, he found, was the prospect Charles Paddon had opened for him. He was, so soon as the opportunity offered, to stay at Trenythan as Charles's friend. Four years ago the fisherman's son returning from his drunken mother's cottage had dreamed of a day, long distant, when naval rank might entitle him to call at the Hall; the dream was to come true sooner than that, and by an unexpected agency.

He looked back over the months of his growing friendship with Paddon to the day he had first stepped on board *Viper*, to Charles's stiff apology and subsequent unbending—a surprising change, that, but not so surprising when you knew Sir Edward Pellew. For it was plain that Pellew's hand was behind the alteration in Paddon's attitude towards him. Yes; he owed a great deal to Edward Pellew.

Not that Jeremiah Coghlan had any idea of resting on these slender, if satisfactory, laurels. The small triumph of *Cerbère*'s cutting-out must be succeeded by other and more resounding deeds, and quickly. And here indeed the prospect was far from bright. That either the Commodore or the defenders of Fort de France would allow him to bring off another cutting-out expedition was unlikely in the extreme, while prolonged blockade duty in *Theseus* was equally unlikely to provide opportunity for gaining distinction. Jeremiah foresaw a dull time ahead even when he had recovered his full strength.

He foresaw correctly, though his vision was limited by ignorance of what was going on in England. Defeat on land had not been compensated for by Nelson's subjugation of Copenhagen. The Government was crumbling. Admiralty was prudently unenterprising, the popular mood was a growing weariness of war. Pitt's successor, with a national majority behind him, made overtures of peace to First Consul Bonaparte. And in November of 1802 the news of the Treaty of Amiens reached the blockading ships of the West Indies squadron. To any aspiring naval officer that news was a blow, and not least to Lieutenant Jeremiah Coghlan, now in possession of his commission and an engraved sword sent to him by Sir John Jervis. When *Theseus* was ordered home to pay off and refit the hope of great deeds had been replaced in his mind by the less noble ambition of establishing himself among the gentry.

CHAPTER SIX

MARGARET

1

Trenythan Hall made no pretensions to the grandeurs of Boconnoc or Lanhydrock, its park being of a dozen acres only and its oak woodlands even less extensive. But the woodlands boasted the oldest oaktree in Cornwall and in the park was a grassy mound which had been the castle of that Paddon ancestor who had been king of Cornwall in the days before history began. So Charles Paddon informed his guest during Jeremiah's first visit to Trenythan in the early Spring of 1802.

Theseus had docked at Portsmouth in January. Her crew were discharged, her officers dispersed. Jeremiah Coghlan found himself without occupation, a lieutenant on half-pay of three shillings a day and no hope of a ship. It was no mere rumour that the Royal Navy was going back to peacetime strength; in the few months since the signing of the Treaty of Amiens 40,000 sailors had been discharged, hundreds of officers relegated to half-pay, and the Grand Fleet at Torbay broken up.

At first Lieutenant Coghlan refused to accept

this unlucky interruption of his sea career, and spent a week in dingy London lodgings while he haunted the Admiralty offices in Whitehall and toured the coffee-houses of the Strand to pick up the latest gossip about the possibility of employment.

Convinced at last that his single exploit in *Viper* weighed nothing at all in a market where the pressure of influence alone counted, he swallowed his new-found pride and resolved to apply for help to his late Commodore. But Sir Edward Pellew was not now accessible through naval channels. It was said that he had abandoned the Navy for politics; that he was to stand for Parliament at Barnstaple in the forthcoming election.

Jeremiah betook himself to Abner Best's little house at Bridport, now his only home, and there tried to forget his frustration in discussing with Abner a possible partnership in the trading activities of the brig *Colombe*. In March Midshipman Paddon had returned home in *Amethyst*, and an enthusiastic letter arrived inviting Jeremiah to visit Trenythan and stay as long as he could.

By this time Jeremiah had accepted that his hope of rising in the Navy was gone; for if this was indeed the end of the war with France it was the end of his prospects of glory and promotion. Charles's letter reminded him that he was in a position to rise by a different ladder, that the gates of Trenythan Hall opened on a new road to that footing among the Gentry which he had insensibly come to look upon as his chief goal.

He could walk now without a stick, and he could ride. Twice he had ridden over to Uploders, a small property with a respectable farmhouse-mansion three miles east of Bridport whose owner wished to sell it. The prize-money from *Cerbère* was enough, though the purchase would leave very little for the maintenance of a gentleman's establishment, and a connection with the Paddons of Trenythan Hall could bring him the status he coveted. Mr Coghlan of Uploders would sound well enough. So he temporised with Abner's suggestion—a coasting brig would be a sorry comedown after the quarterdeck of a 74—and wrote accepting Charles Paddon's invitation.

The letter of reply required much consideration and heart-searching. It was one thing to have contracted a friendship in the wartime ardours of an armed cutter on foreign service, quite another to pursue it into the unknown territory of the landed gentry. Jeremiah had learned the manners and modes that would pass him as a gentleman with any officer of the Royal Navy but at Trenythan he would have to encounter (among other trials) the company of ladies—Lady Paddon and Charles's twin sister, perhaps others. His courage came near to failing him at the thought. In the end he wrote that he would come to Trenythan on March 20th but that 'urgent business connected with property' would necessitate his returning by the 24th. With his retreat thus assured, he made the two-day coach journey by way of Exeter and Plymouth to Liskeard, where he hired a nag for the eighteen miles to Trenythan. At dusk of a cold and blustery day he rode in through the gates of Trenythan Hall and up the avenue of leafless oaks to the big old house.

If Jeremiah's apprehensions had been of pomp and stateliness they were quickly dispelled. True, his heart leaped into his mouth when the huge oaken door was opened, for the old man who opened it was a Polruan man remembered from his youth; but the servant did not recognise him, and when Charles Paddon came jumping down the great staircase into the hall to greet him the warmth of his friend's welcome drove such ignoble fears from his mind.

'This is the best thing that's happened since Fort de France! How's the leg? Have you got a ship? Did Tom take your horse?' Charles interrupted his spate of questions to shout peremptorily. 'Tom! Where the devil are you? Mr Coghlan's beast to the stables, and look lively. Henry,' he added to the old servant, 'tell Sue to bring hot water to the tower room. Come on, Jerry—you're to go aloft but there's stairs instead of ratlines.'

There was a fire in the fireplace of the tower room and a tent-bed with carved posts and tester. And a log-fire blazed in the vast fireplace of the room to which he descended half-an-hour later in his new blue coat and white breeches, to be presented by Charles to Lady Paddon, a faded lady in powder and velvet who peered myopically at him and welcomed him kindly and without condescension. The old lady in the big chair close to the fire, she explained to him, was her mother, Lady Lavery, and she was stone-deaf so Mr Coghlan had better not try to converse with her. Jeremiah made his bow to a very old person in a lace cap who seemed to be clothed entirely in shawls and returned him a nod. Then a servant in livery brought glasses of spiced wine and they sat talking very pleasantly, Charles doing most of it, until a servant—yet another one—entered to announce that dinner was served.

It had taken only this short period for Jeremiah's nervousness to be banished entirely. Already he felt at home in Trenythan, though it was unlike any home he had ever known. Here was no glittering pretension of wealth but a richness of comfort and stability; an age-old assurance that accepted servants and fires and easy well-ordered living without question, without pride or display. Matters go on here, the old house seemed to say, as they have been since time began and will be until time ends. The feeling that he belonged here warmed him (perhaps not unassisted by the spiced wine) as he went into the lofty dining-room with Lady Paddon on his arm. And within a minute this pleasant warmth was lost in the hot flame of a new and stranger sensation. He saw Margaret.

She came in quickly with a rustle of silk skirts, to be chided gently for her lateness by Lady Paddon and answer with some laughing excuse. Charles gave her a frown and made a hurried business of presenting his guest, for they had been on the point of sitting at table. Jeremiah, bowing as the girl curtseyed, saw loveliness that made him catch his breath.

She was dark and slim like her brother and the close likeness was there, but Charles's good looks were in her rounded and tinted into warm beauty. The big dark eyes that looked up for a moment into his held frankness and laughter. Their glance set his head spinning and he had some ado to get himself without clumsiness into the chair a footman held for him.

After that the evening passed, for Jeremiah, like some rosy but bewildering dream. He was dimly conscious of eating and drinking, of some sort of conversation with Lady Paddon on his left, of old Lady Lavery on his right apparently *incommunicado* over a bowl of bread-and-milk. In reply to a question from Charles he managed to produce an account of the food and company in *Theseus*'s wardroom. But the vivid awareness of Margaret opposite to him across the table was like a bright mist enveloping his senses and befogging his mind and he knew his words were stumbling and ill-chosen. The light from a dozen candles in the chandelier above the table dwelt softly on ivory shoulders half revealed by the lace of her claret-coloured gown and glinted on the dark ringlets that hung nearly to the smooth curves of her bosom. When she spoke, which was not often, her voice was low and sweet; unlike the hard ringing tones of her brother, who was just now deploring the lost chance of promotion.

'But you'll go to sea again soon, Mr Coghlan?' asked Margaret. 'They'll surely find you a ship?'

Her glance was frank and kind. For Jeremiah it was a stab that left him in confusion and made reply an effort.

'I—I hardly think so. Indeed, I've no hope of it.'

'What will you do, then?'

He felt her warmth of interest and responded with more confidence. 'Turn landsman, Miss Paddon. I think of purchasing a house and land and—well, cultivating turnips.'

Margaret laughed; and Jeremiah felt he could listen to such music for ever.

'From topsails to turnips is a sad fall,' she

said.

'And a damnable—I beg pardon, mother—a shocking waste,' said Charles. 'If you'd seen Jerry slashing away that night in the Fort de France anchorage—'

He launched into an account of the *Cerbère* cutting-out expedition that brought dark colour into his late commander's cheeks and admiring glances from his sister.

'But despite that terrible wound you walk as well as you did before it,' she said later when they were seated round the fire in the withdrawing room.

'Not precisely,' Jeremiah said. 'I must always limp, they tell me.'

'No one would notice it. I don't. And I fancy it would not prevent you from dancing.' Margaret turned to her mother. 'On the seventeenth, mamma—don't you agree?'

Lady Paddon blinked at her and blinked at Jeremiah. 'Oh, of course. Mr Coghlan's present visit is much too short, I protest.'

'That's it,' exclaimed Charles, who was standing with an elbow on the mantelpiece. 'A week at least next time, and seventeenth May in the middle of it.'

'It's our birthday,' Margaret explained. 'Charles's and mine. There'll be a small party here—and you must make one in it, Mr Coghlan—and a few guests more for dancing on the seventeenth. You will come, won't you?'

Her eyes said plainly that she wanted him to come. He couldn't doubt it and the certainty bemused him. He stammered awkwardly that he was honoured, that he feared he would make but a clumsy dancer, that circumstances had afforded him little opportunity—until Lady Paddon, taking pity on him, said kindly that it was to be a prodigious informal affair and she considered Mr Coghlan engaged for it.

Lying in his comfortable tent-bed that night Mr Coghlan found sleep hard to come by. His mind was a turmoil of thoughts in which Margaret, laughing or grave or swaying gracefully in her wine-coloured gown, hovered persistently. Nothing like this had happened to him before. It had been quite different with Susan Cargis; with relief he remembered Abner telling him of her marriage to a Looe stonemason. As for the girl in Portsmouth and that Jamaican quadroon at Kingston—he thrust them hastily out of his mind, feeling ashamed and slightly sick at the recollection. Margaret was a world away from these things. Far above them, yes; and yet not a goddess inaccessible, for she had shown—surely he couldn't be mistaken—that she liked him. Or was it possibly the ordinary kindness a Paddon of Trenythan would show to a guest, her brother's friend? In a confusion of hopes and doubts he fell at last asleep.

The dull March weather was at least dry for

the morning's tour of Trenythan with Charles as his conductor. They spent much time in the stables, where two grooms and a stableman assisted in the selection of a solid-looking bay as a suitable mount for Jeremiah (they would ride out tomorrow, declared Charles) and more in the mossy graveyard beside the little chapel in the park.

Jeremiah felt some discomfort as his companion led him from one mouldering stone to another discoursing the while on the deeds of Paddons dead and gone. There was a depth of pride in ancestry here that recalled Charles's outburst on the stormwswept deck of *Indefatigable* five years ago; not for the first time, Jeremiah experienced a stir of wonder at the change that had brought the dogmatist of Blood into friendship with a fellow so humbly born as himself. But Charles seemed unaware of his uneasiness.

Margaret came with them on a walk after luncheon to exercise the dogs, two beagles, a couple of terriers, and a half-trained setter. This was not in accordance with her brother's plans.

'Jerry and I are taking 'em across Lampetho marshes,' he said with a frown when she joined them. ''Tisn't a walk for you, Margaret.'

Margaret wrinkled her nose at him. She was dressed in a grey pelisse trimmed with black fur and the biting wind made her cheeks pink as wild-rose petals.

'All walks are for me, dear brother,' she said. 'I see you don't want me—but does Mr Coghlan?'

'I do,' said Jeremiah, with an emphasis as unexpected as it was unintentional.

'Your obliged servant, sir.' She dropped him a mock curtsey. 'There, Charles. I vote with the "ayes" so it's two votes to one and I'm coming.'

Charles shrugged. 'You don't take me for a democrat, I hope. Very well—come along. Rip! Heel, you scoundrels!'

They set off across the grass of the park at a great pace, Margaret with the young setter on lead. He was, she told Jeremiah breathlessly, her own dog, named Stroke because he pulled so hard. Pull he did as the three walked and trotted briskly over rough turf and then downhill through oakwoods, treading the crisp gold of dead leaves under the bare waving branches. When rabbit-scent excited the smaller dogs in front to a furious barking and Stroke tugged madly at his lead Jeremiah reached for the lead and caught Margaret's hand. The movement brought their bodies in contact.

'I'll take him,' he said; his voice was not quite steady.

The girl looked at him quickly. Her dark eyes held no laughter and she said nothing as she surrendered the lead.

They came down to the fringe of the woods,

where the flat marsh stretched in reeds and low thickets to the leaden sheen of the sea beyond Parr Sands. The dogs plunged madly after startled waterfowl, there was jumping and splashing and laughter, there was more than one occasion for Jeremiah to take Margaret's hand and swing her across the half-frozen runnels. Then up through the oakwoods by a little path from the seaward end of the marsh, with a saffron bar of sunset fading through the skein of branches behind them. Margaret had taken Stroke's lead again and Charles was ahead with the beagles and terriers. There came sudden pandemonium of barking, a cry of 'Fox!' and a view-hallo from Charles, and the setter lunged forward pulling his mistress to the ground. She was up, laughing, before Jeremiah could spring to her aid.

'No, of course I'm not hurt one bit,' she said, answering his anxious question. 'Pray don't look so tragically alarmed, Mr Coghlan. But you may take the lead, if you can do so without grabbing as you did last time.'

'I count it a privilege, Miss Paddon,' Jeremiah said. 'To hold Stroke's lead, that is. Not to grab.'

Margaret smiled quickly at him and led the way up the path.

'You'll not be offended, Mr Coghlan,' she said over her shoulder, 'if I say I'm tired of calling you "Mr Coghlan". It's not—forgive me—a pretty name. Charles calls you Jerry—'

'Which also isn't a pretty name.'

'Better than Jeremiah. I hope you'll allow me to call you Jerry.'

'Charles calls you Margaret,' said Jeremiah boldly.

'He calls me Peg as often as not,' she said without looking round. 'But I'd prefer Margaret from you, Jerry.'

'Look lively, there!' shouted Charles, waiting for them on the hill-brow. 'Clap on sail or we'll not be in before dusk.'

That was the first of two golden days. They rode on the second day, a clear morning and afternoon of early Spring sunshine, by fields and downs inland. Charles on a spirited three-year-old, spent most of the time several furlongs ahead, and Jeremiah was more than content to sit his bay with Margaret for company, laughing and lovely in a dark-red habit. By the ancient mound of Castle Dore they rode, and past Caruggat Wood and down the steep tracks to Luxulyan in the glen for a nooning of beef and ale at the inn there. Then up over Crift Downs to the Logan Rock above Red Moor before turning for home.

It was a long enough day for the horses but not long enough for Jeremiah, who was regretting his earlier insistence on returning to Bridport by the 24th. With Margaret he was completely happy; it was as if he had known her all his life. But she, he realised with a qualm, had not known him until three days ago—did not know him now. And she was a Paddon of Trenythan.

It was dusk when they rode in at Trenythan gates and handed over the horses to the grooms. Charles lingered at the stables, arguing about the three-year-old's saddle with the head groom, and Jeremiah and Margaret walked slowly together towards the house. Jeremiah halted suddenly and she turned inquiringly.

'Margaret,' he said; and stopped.

'Well, Jerry?' It was too dark to see her face but he knew she was smiling. 'I know you have something to say, but I can't help you, you know.'

He went at it doggedly. There must be no pretence with her, of all people in the world.

'Charles knows this but you don't. I'm not gentry born, Margaret. My father—he's dead long ago—was a fisherman in Polruan. There's no drop of gentle blood—'

'Jerry.' She stopped him with a hand on his arm. 'You've no need to tell me this. Do you think I care? Charles nurses this foolishness about the blood of the Paddons—his father did, and his grandfather—but I don't. If I like someone it doesn't matter to me who his father was. And you—' She checked herself quickly. 'Here comes Charles. And I must tell Sue to heat water for our tubs.'

She gathered up the skirt of her habit and ran to the house. Jeremiah, following more slowly with Charles, listened to an exposition of the merits and demerits of the English hunting saddle without hearing a word.

He was away next morning before sun-up to catch the coach at Liskeard. Charles came down to see him off and so (unexpectedly) did Margaret, swathed from neck to ankle in a fur-trimmed gown and with her dark hair hastily piled on her small head. The warm touch of her hand, the music of her voice reminding him that he was to return to Trenythan in May, stayed with him all the long way back to Bridport.

2

'If we don't make a stand now we face disaster—that's the long and short of it.' Lord Delamere refilled his glass with port and passed the decanter to Charles Paddon on his left. 'Boney's all set to bully the world into submission.'

Across the table Sir George Penberthy's bulging blue eyes surveyed him incredulously. 'But God damn me, we've been at peace six months and more!' he puffed. 'How the devil can we have at 'em now, with half an army and half a navy left?'

'We'll just have to, sir, and that's certain,' said Delamere. 'I tell you I was in Paris five weeks ago and there was damned little talk of peace there. I watched Bonaparte reviewing one of his armies in front of the Tuileries. I talked with the Comte de Missiessy of their navy. They're building warships in every port from the Scheldt to Biscay.'

Sir George snorted. 'Oh come now, my lord—he didn't tell you that?'

'Boasted of it, sir. Where's the need for secrecy when they intend to bludgeon us into accepting Boney's broken treaties and stolen territories?' Delamere gulped port and leaned across the table, his square ruddy face flushed. 'Look at Switzerland and Piedmont—grabbed while Whitworth lapped up the First Consul's talk of a permanent peace. Look at Malta—'

Jeremiah ceased to listen to a conversation which could not engage his attention. From beyond the dining-room door came the sounds of fiddles tuning and the murmur of voices as the after-dinner guests arrived for the ball that was to celebrate the birthday of Charles and Margaret Paddon. In a few minutes he would see Margaret again; perhaps touch her hand in the dance. He gulped nervously, remembering the few lessons he had taken from an *emigré* Frenchman in Bridport and the clumsiness of his right leg.

The ladies had left the six men—Charles and

the five male guests who were staying at Trenythan Hall—to their port. Sir George Penberthy, a distant cousin, had come over the previous night from Crewkerne, and there were two young squires from north Cornwall, Trenear and Westlake, whose attentions to Margaret had been a good deal too marked for Jeremiah's liking. As for Delamere, Lord Delamere since his father's death but otherwise little changed from *Indefatigable*'s midshipman of five years ago, Jeremiah had been glad to meet him again; but his pleasure in their talk of past days afloat had been only half-hearted. The Navy and all things appertaining to it were of little moment when Margaret occupied all his thoughts, filled all his horizon.

'Then if Lord Delamere's right we'd best look to swords and pistols,' Trenear was saying; he was a handsome fellow, wearing his saffron coat and ruffled stock with an air. 'They'll be mustering the Yeomanry again—eh, Sir George?'

'No doubt, sir, no doubt.' Sir George pursed his lips. 'That is, if the Government makes a move. I can't see them moving, myself.'

'Well, whether they move or not, we'd better,' said Charles, standing up. 'The fiddlers are striking up, gentlemen. Let's join the ladies.'

They went through into the farther room, a large and lofty chamber ablaze with the light from four big chandeliers and thronged with people—forty or fifty guests, Jeremiah thought. There was no fire in the great fireplace, for the May night was warm, and the three fiddles and bass viol who occupied a place there were scraping away at the opening bars of dance music.

Jeremiah looked eagerly for Margaret among the flowered satins and dress coats, but he was too late. The three sets for the quadrille, which were all the floor space allowed, were already made up and Trenear was partnering Margaret in one of the eights. Delamere, he saw, was standing opposite a pretty girl in one of the other sets. He made his way round the room to where Lady Paddon was sitting with old Lady Lavery dozing at her side. Margaret's mother peered somewhat disconcertingly at him and then apologised for her shortsightedness.

'It makes me slow to recognise even my friends,' she said with her faint, kindly smile. 'But I fancy you also, Mr Coghlan, have been a little slow. They tell me that Harry Trenear is Margaret's partner for this first dance.'

Jeremiah, inwardly elated by the suggestion that he had been expected to partner Margaret, sought hastily for a polite rejoinder.

'At least I may be beforehand now, ma'am. May I have the honour of your—that is, will you honour me by—'

He failed miserably to find the proper form of

words and Lady Paddon helped him out.

'If you're asking me to partner you in the next dance, Mr Coghlan, I fear I must decline. 'Tis to be a country-dance, I understand, and I'm not sufficiently nimble. But ask Margaret—and be first this time.'

Jeremiah's dancing-lessons had not included the country-dance.

'I think I may not be sufficiently nimble myself, ma'am,' he said.

'Margaret will see you through it,' said Lady Paddon placidly. 'Ask her, Mr Coghlan—she will be displeased if you don't, I know.'

Jeremiah answered her small confidential smile with a bow. His heart was beating fast. This was encouragement indeed for an enterprise which he still felt to be too lofty for him. The quadrille was well under way now, and he watched the lively figures in silence for some time. Trenear, opposite Margaret, was displaying a graceful ingenuity of step which he could never hope to equal and he felt a pang of jealousy; then he saw the quick turning of Margaret's head as she glanced about her as if seeking someone, and her smile when she caught sight of himself and ceased her search, and had no more envy of Trenear.

'Eight bars more and they make an end,' said Lady Paddon, tapping his arm. 'Mr Coghlan, I release you.'

He slipped quickly through the folk standing

at the edge of the dance floor and was within a few paces of Margaret when the quadrille ended with bows and courtesies. He bowed as she came towards him on Trenear's arm.

'Thank you, Harry,' she was saying, 'but I'm trysted with Tom for the next quadrille. Go and talk to mamma like a good boy.—You didn't dance, Jerry?' she added as Trenear moved reluctantly away.

'I don't want to dance with anyone but you,' said Jeremiah; he offered his arm and she placed her hand on it. 'Will you be my partner next time?'

She was wearing a white gown, high-waisted and cut so low that he could see the valley between her small breasts. A black ringlet hung to touch one bare shoulder.

'It's a country-dance, you know,' she warned him.

'I know—and I've to confess that I've never danced a country-dance before.'

'You recommend yourself very oddly, Mr Coghlan,' she mocked him. '"Pray dance with me, ma'am, though I cannot dance".'

'I'm sorry,' said Jeremiah, downcast. 'Perhaps I should have asked for the next quadrille. I assure you I can—'

'No, no, sir. You heard me say that I'm engaged for the quadrille. We'll country-dance together, and I will be your guide.' Her dark eyes looked up into his. 'Do you think you can manage, with me to help you?'

'I think I could do anything in the world with you to help me,' he said, low-voiced.

She turned her head away swiftly but he saw the quick heave of her breast. The fiddles sounded a loud chord.

'They're starting!' cried Margaret excitedly. 'Come on!—And Jerry, watch what the others do and look to me when you're stuck.'

She pulled him into a laughing circle of men and girls and the dance began. It was a frolicsome affair with less emphasis on graceful footwork than the quadrille, and by keeping his wits on the alert for the course followed by the preceding couples, and his eye on Margaret for signals, Jeremiah managed creditably enough. The galloping step required by the figures of the dance was no trial to his limping foot, and there were others beside himself who amid shouts and laughter had now and then to be pushed into their proper course. And there were moments of delight when he and Margaret whirled with tight-clasped hands in the centre of the circle or trotted hand-in-hand between the ranks of their fellow-dancers.

At the end of it there was an outburst of clapping and jocular shouting, with everyone flushed and breathless. Jeremiah found himself being steered to the outskirts of the throng with Margaret's hand tightly clasped on his arm.

'That—was—wonderful,' she panted. 'But

oh—I'm so heated, Jerry. Let's go outside and breathe fresh air. The door at the end, behind the screen.'

They came out onto a flagged terrace that ran along the side of the house and paced there slowly, her hand still resting on his arm. The night was moonless but warm and very still, scented with early lilac and a faint tang of the sea. A multitude of stars gave a blue radiance that contrasted with the golden bars of light that fell across the stones from the long chinks between the window curtains, bars that intermittently gilded Margaret's white dress and smooth shoulders as they walked. Neither of them spoke for a little while, and when the girl broke the silence her voice sounded forced and artificial.

'Country-dances are much more fun than quadrilles. Don't you agree?'

'I've small experience of either.' Jeremiah's tone, too, was oddly stilted. 'The next is a quadrille—and you're engaged for it, I remember.'

'With Tom Westlake—but Tom's a boor and he's had too much to drink. I shall break the engagement.'

'Then you don't think I'm a boor, Margaret?'

'If I did, Jerry, would I be out here with you now? Tom, now—oh, Tom's very well in his way, but he'd be sure to try to kiss me.'

'And what would you do then?' asked

Jeremiah gravely.

'Why, I'd slap his face,' cried Margaret fiercely.

'Oh.'

They had reached the end of the terrace and turned to pace back again. Jeremiah halted and turned, taking both the girl's hands in his.

'If I kissed you, Margaret,' he said, 'would you slap my face?'

The windows threw no light here but he could see the shine of starlight in her eyes as they looked up at him.

'I—I don't know,' she whispered. 'But—'

Then she was in his arms and his mouth was hard and hungry against her parted lips. For a moment her body was soft and yielding in his embrace before she thrust herself away. Jeremiah caught at her hand and held it.

'I should—slap your face, I suppose,' she said tremulously.

'Margaret!' he said with sudden urgency. 'With me this is serious—the most important thing in my life. I love you. I believe you know that. And you—' He checked, raging inwardly at his lack of words, his poverty in fine phrases to fit this high moment. 'Can I hope—dare I hope that you can return my love?'

'I don't know,' she said a second time, after a moment. 'Let me go, Jerry.'

He tightened his grasp as she tried to free her hand. 'Answer me only this, Margaret. Will you accept—' he stumbled again over the words—'will you allow me to—to pay my addresses to you? Accept me as your lover?'

She gave a little gasping laugh. 'I don't take—lovers, sir.'

'I'm not jesting!' he cried harshly; and then more softly, 'You know my meaning, my dear. Will you give me your answer?'

'Loose my hand first,' said Margaret.

When he had obeyed she stood facing him in the darkness for a breathing-space. Then—

'Yes,' she whispered, and turned from him to run along the terrace and in by the house door.

Jeremiah did not follow her. For a long time he stood where he was, gazing unseeing at the starry sky in a kind of ecstasy. At the back of his mind a doubt or two stirred uncomfortably: Charles Paddon's reaction to this happening; his own prospects or lack of them. But these things seemed negligible beside the towering triumph of his love and he gave them no conscious thought. Yet there was one thing (equally negligible, he would have said contemptuously) that added itself willy-nilly to his delight. Jeremiah Coghlan had won not only his Margaret but also the daughter of Sir John Paddon of Trenythan. The upward step was made, his place in society assured.

When at last he went unobtrusively in by the house door it was to find the last dance ending and the older guests talking of having their carriages to the door. Servants brought wine, Charles and Margaret were toasted in a final stirrup-cup (Jeremiah joining the acclamations from the fringe of the encircling throng) and the party began to disperse. He had a touch of the hand and a quick glance from Margaret before she retired, and a heartening scowl from Trenear. Declining a pressing invitation from Delamere to join in a game of hazard, Jeremiah paid his respects to Lady Paddon and went up to his room, to bed but not to sleep.

The problems of the future, easy enough to thrust aside when he had stood in bemused rapture under the stars, came upon him with more force as he lay tossing restlessly under Trenythan roof. He could buy Uploders and take Margaret there when they were married, but the house had nothing about it that resembled Trenythan Hall with its comforts and servants and settled ease.

He would have to work, and work hard, before they could afford a carriage, for instance—and Margaret would have to work too. He was sure now that she loved him; but he was uncertain—and the uncertainty troubled him—that her love would stand the burdens that must fall upon the wife of an impoverished farmer-squire.

There would, he supposed, be some dowry to come with his bride, but the Paddons were not great landowners and presumably not over-wealthy. And there was the question of her brother. Charles's prejudices in the matter of blood had not prevented him from making a friend and companion of the fisherman's son. But would he welcome the fisherman's son as his brother-in-law? Charles was the head of the family. He could refuse to permit the marriage. And then there was Lady Paddon, who seemed to favour his attachment to Margaret but was (presumably) ignorant of his origins . . .

Jeremiah, turning and turning again on his soft bed, revolved these things until his feverish thoughts tangled themselves in a hopeless confusion and the darkness of his room paled into the grey of dawn. He set himself resolutely to get some sleep; but the sleep that had always come so easily in the comfortless berths of his seagoing years could not be won on the down mattress of Trenythan Hall. At last, with sunrise less than an hour away, he got up, splashed water from the ewer on his face, and dressed himself. There had been talk of a ride with Charles and Margaret that morning, so he put on the coat and breeches in which he had ridden over from Liskeard, and carrying his boots in his hand tiptoed down the stairs. No one was yet astir. Unwilling to risk the noise he might make in drawing the bolts of the great door in the hall, he made his way to the room of last night's dancing and went out by the little door onto the terrace.

The sky of early morning was clear and radiant with growing light, and a ceaseless thrill of bird-song filled the air. He drew in the freshness of the new day in thirsty draughts, standing on the very flagstone (he identified it reverently) where he had held Margaret in his arms only half-a-dozen hours ago. The doubts and problems of the night fled before that remembrance. All would come right; Margaret was his and the rest was nothing beside that. He pulled his boots on and stepped across dewy grass, his face uplifted to an eastern heaven now flushing with rose, the mirror of his own rosy future.

Earthy scents of dung and urine made him aware that his aimless course had brought him to the entrance of the stable-yard, and he decided to take a look at the horses—the bay he would ride that morning and the hack he had hired in Liskeard. The half-door of one of the loose stalls was open, and as he crossed the cobbles Charles Paddon looked out of it. Charles still wore the laced coat he had worn for the dance, and his eyes were bleary and red-rimmed. Jeremiah gave him good morning.

'You're up betimes,' he added.

'Haven't been to bed,' Charles growled; he came out and closed the half-door. 'Sat don't know how many hours at hazard and lost twenty guineas. Head like a damned beehive. You're up early yourself.'

'I couldn't sleep.'

Charles had to be told, and the sooner it was over with the better. Jeremiah drew a deep breath.

'Charles.' Between happiness and apprehension his voice emerged as a squeak and he began again. 'Charles, I've news for you. Good news, I hope. Margaret and I—I'm the most fortunate of men, Charles. Margaret returns my love. I want to marry her. I must ask your permission, of course—and I've told her I'm a fisherman's son and she said she cared nothing for that.'

He saw that Paddon's unshaven jaw had dropped and that his eyes were wide and staring, but he took it for mere astonishment and babbled on.

'It was last night, Charles, out here. On the flagged terrace. We came out after the country-dance—'

'Stop!' Charles shouted the word in a high unnatural voice. 'It's impossible—impossible!'

Jeremiah's brows drew together. 'You refuse your permission?'

'You damn fool, it's not that. No, by God—it's I that's been the fool. I should have guessed this might happen. You can't marry Margaret, Jerry. She's your half-sister.'

For a moment Jeremiah stood rigid, unmoving, his expression giving no sign that he had heard.

'My father was your father,' said Paddon loudly. 'You and I are brothers by blood. That's why—'

'*No!*'

Jeremiah shrank back on the word as if he had been struck. The denial struck a flash of anger from his friend.

'I say yes, damn you! D'ye think I don't know? Pellew told me two years ago and he'd made certain of it. I thought you'd have tumbled to it by now. Why d'ye think I've given you my friendship, the friendship of a Paddon, these past months? When you took command of *Viper*—'

Jeremiah, stunned and stupefied by the blow, heard Charles's voice imperfectly, as from a great distance. But those last words made an impact, and sent a series of blurred pictures fleeting through his mind: *Viper*'s after-cabin and Charles's inexplicable change towards him; Abner Best at the Bridport inn, prevaricating about Sir Edward's visit; Pellew himself, at their first meeting—*something the look of an old acquaintance, long dead*, and Pellew, as Charles had once told him, had known Sir John Paddon. And his mother, too; that last scene in the Polruan cottage came back to him, and some words spoken in her drunken tones made sense. There was no room for doubt. It was true.

With a great effort he made himself stand

erect amid the ruins of his shattered world. His voice was harsh and even when he spoke, and Charles Paddon gave back a step before the grim fixity of his expression.

'You should have told me this before,' he said coldly.

'I—Pellew said not to, Jerry,' Paddon stammered. 'It seems that fellow Best asked him to keep mum about it. For God, if I'd known—'

'You will tell her yourself what you've told me,' Jeremiah went on as if he had not spoken. 'I shall leave Trenythan at once. Now. We shall not meet again.'

'But see here—'

'I ask a service of you, Charles, a last service. Please to saddle my horse. I'll get my dunnage from the house.'

He turned and limped away across the yard, leaving Charles Paddon staring after him with a hand clutching his unkempt black hair.

3

Of the journey back to Bridport Jeremiah's memory afterwards retained little or nothing. His seething thoughts were turned inward, dwelling in painful repetition on the simple facts of his catastrophe. He had lost Margaret. His aspirations to gentility were dead, killed at a blow. And he was a bastard; Abner Best had known that from the first. That was why Abner had taken Sir John Paddon's by-blow away from Polruan with its Methody bigots. He could feel no gratitude for that now, only unreasoning hatred for all who had conspired to steer him onto the rock that had wrecked his life.

As for Margaret, remembrance of her brought such exquisite pain that he felt he must go mad if it persisted. Bringing all his will to bear, he tried to force her out of his mind, out of his life. But the light of dark eyes, the curve of smooth breasts, the feel of her softness in his arms, haunted him through the morning ride to Liskeard and the weary jolting of the Plymouth coach.

At the inns and post-houses there was excited talk and even cheering, but he was deaf to it and oblivious of its cause. The ostler who brought his hack at the White Hart in Exeter was full of news, but it died on his lips at sight of the grim countenance that confronted him. It was late, a windy starlit night, when Jeremiah reached Bridport. He came into East Street and turned his tired nag in at the gate of the Greyhound inn's stable-yard. Though it was past midnight every window of the inn shone with lamplight and a din of shouting and singing issued from its open door, but no one came in answer to his shouts.

He tethered the horse to a ring in the wall, unstrapped his portmanteau, and went round to the door. Two men were coming out, one supporting the other, and he collided with them.

'Blast ye for a clumsy bugger!' hiccupped the supporter. 'Why the—well, damn me if 'taint Muster C-Coghlan. Beg p-pardon, sir, surely—and ye come right handily, now. Lend a hand, will ye, wi' Cap'n Best.'

'Abner Best—drunk?' demanded Jeremiah incredulously; he had never known his adoptive father the worse for liquor.

'Pissed as a soused herring, sir. The war, ye see. We've been drinking damnation to the French these four hours, every man of us.'

'We're at war again—with France?' Jeremiah said dazedly.

'Aye. Ye've not heard? News came this morning. Help me get the cap'n home, will ye, sir.'

'Take my portmanteau.' Jeremiah stooped to get his shoulder under Abner's limp body and hoisted him on his back. 'Bring it down to the house.'

A corner of the black cloud that had lain across his mind lifted itself and he saw beneath it. Life, another and familiar life, still stretched ahead after all. As he limped down the cobbled street with his burden the breath of salt air came tangily to his nostrils and he seemed to hear sounds he had almost forgotten: the surge of waves along a ship's side, the creak and rustle of cordage and canvas, the boom of cannon.

'Ye'll be off to sea again, Muster Coghlan,' said the fellow trotting beside him.

'Yes,' said Jeremiah between his teeth. 'I'll be off to sea again.'

CHAPTER SEVEN

MASTER AND COMMANDER

1

Rear-Admiral Richard Dacres, Commander-in-Chief of His Majesty's Ships and Vessels in the West Indies, gestured imperatively at his Negro footman, who obediently proffered the dish of fruit to the Admiral's guest. Lord Henry Leveson declined with a word and a smile and Dacres dismissed the man with a wave of the hand.

'You'll sup on board *Renard*, no doubt,' he said. 'I trust you won't starve before you reach Bridgetown, Lord Henry. Her captain—Coghlan's his name—has something of a Spartan reputation where food's concerned.'

'I expect I shall do very well,' said Lord Henry placidly.

He was short and plump in contrast to his host's six feet of leanness, and his round and amiable countenance was topped by a neatly-ordered thatch of silvery hair. Occasionally the Jamaican sea-breeze, flitting in through the open but shaded windows of the Admiral's hillside residence, stirred fine wisps of hair to waver comically upright from Lord Henry's head, and then he would raise a pudgy hand to pat them gently back into place.

'This vessel the *Renard*,' he went on, 'is called a ship-sloop, I understand. She is a small ship, then?'

'By comparison with *Theseus*, yes.' Dacres frowned. 'As I've said, I regret I'm unable to send you to Barbados in *Theseus*, which would be more suitable to your dignity as Governor. But the situation in the West Indies, Lord Henry, requires every seventy-four I can muster for the proposed attack on San Domingo. How their Lordships expect me to do anything against the French with four of the line and a brace of frigates I cannot imagine. It's more than three years since the war was renewed, and here's Martinique and Guadeloupe and half-a-dozen other islands still in French hands. And even with *Theseus* I've few enough for this San Domingo expedition—'

His high voice rambled peevishly on while Lord Henry listened with half an ear, his face wearing its customary expression of mild contentment which masked a mind shrewd and experienced in men and affairs. He had come out from England in *Theseus* to take up his appointment as Governor of Barbados; four thousand miles, half of them stormy, had not disturbed his equanimity and the onward voyage of another thousand in a smaller vessel gave him no concern.

'Pray understand that I make not the least complaint, sir,' he said as soon as he could get a word in. 'I shall be very happy to make the voyage in *Renard*. Captain Bligh of *Theseus* told me she bears a high reputation in the Caribbean.'

'Oh, she's a smart enough vessel,' Dacres said grudgingly. 'Brings in prizes, French and Dutch, after every cruise. Coghlan's trained his crew well, I'll say that for him. He's Captain Coghlan by courtesy, you understand, Lord Henry—holds the rank of Master and Commander.' The Admiral's thin lips curled slightly. 'Climbed to the quarterdeck after coming in through the hawse-hole.'

'Indeed?'

'A *protégé* of Pellew's, I'm told. I've no time for these jumped-up admiral's pets, sir. At any rate, Mr Coghlan's patron is t'other side the world, C-in-C East Indies, so he can look for no favours—' the Admiral caught himself up sharply and showed some embarrassment. 'But I must beg pardon, Lord Henry. I believe

Admiral Pellew is a friend of yours.'

'We were at school together,' nodded Lord Henry, 'and we keep up a desultory correspondence. Tell me, Admiral—I am deplorably ignorant in such matters—how long will this voyage to Barbados occupy?'

'The south-easters are blowing in the eastern Caribbean, which means you won't have a fair wind. I'd say twelve days to a fortnight, given no untoward encounters with the French.'

'You think we may encounter enemy ships?' inquired Lord Henry interestedly.

Dacres shrugged. 'A long chance of it. A possibility, no more. Privateers out of St Pierre or Pointe à Pitre—they're the bane of our merchant shipping and I can't spare frigates to cope with them. Coghlan caught one of 'em a month ago and trounced her soundly. I wish he'd catch that fellow Arbos.'

'Arbos? A Spanish name, I think.'

'It could be,' said Dacres. 'He wears French colours. Calls his ship *General Ernouf* after the governor of Guadeloupe—and that's a damned insult, for she was the Royal Navy ship-sloop *Lily* until a French privateer captured her.'

Lord Henry patted his wind-blown hair. 'A ship-sloop, you say. Then should she accost *Renard* we should give a good account of ourselves.'

'But you won't,' the Admiral said with a laugh. 'Coghlan will have strict orders to avoid all engagement with the enemy.' He stood up and made a bow. 'His most valuable passenger must not be put at risk. Shall we go out on the terrace? This room grows too hot.'

When they were seated in cane armchairs on the terrace, which was shaded by an awning, a black servant brought cigars. The awning flapped in the warm breeze, but the hedge of shrubs ablaze with tropical flowers gave shelter from the wind; beyond and below lay Kingston harbour, shimmering blue under the glare of the afternoon sky. Lord Henry drew a watch from his fob.

'I believe I am to go on board in two hours' time,' he said.

'My carriage is ordered for you, Lord Henry.' The Admiral waved his cigar in a deprecatory gesture. 'You'll not object to sharing with your manservant, I trust?'

'Not the least, sir. Carberry and I are old travelling companions, not to say incorrigible gossips. I believe we have exchanged, over the years, every detail of our respective life-stories.'

Admiral Dacres looked slightly disgusted. 'You may be thrown upon one another's society in *Renard*,' he remarked, with that unpleasant curl of the lip. 'Jeremiah Coghlan's the most unsociable devil that ever wore an epaulette. Maybe he's more at ease on the lower deck.'

'Be that as it may,' said Lord Henry, 'Captain Coghlan and I are like to be thrown together, so to speak, during a voyage of two weeks in a small vessel. It would be as well, perhaps, if I knew a little about him before we meet.'

'Little enough to tell.' Dacres flicked the ash from his cigar impatiently. 'He was second in *Vanguard* and did well in the action with *Seduisant*—Duckworth gave him his present command. He's a good enough seaman, but mad.'

'Mad?' Lord Henry was mildly astonished.

'Mad on gunnery. *Renard* expends more powder and shot than any ship in my command—and ninety per cent of it, mark you, on gun practice.'

'Oh. Is he married?'

'No. And the buzz is he don't give a damn for women. And he's ambitious, like all these would-be gentry. Give his soul for a post-captaincy, I don't doubt—but he won't get it in the Caribbean. The Mediterranean and the Spanish waters are the places for promotion just now.'

'Of course,' Lord Henry agreed. 'That is the arena of decision, as you say. And unless I'm much mistaken the gladiators are arming at this moment.'

'The glad—? Ah, I take you.' The Admiral nodded sagely. 'Villeneuve and the Spanish admiral—Gravina, I fancy it will be—*versus* Nelson. But I think you said Nelson was on shore?'

'He came ashore in August, a week before I sailed in *Theseus*,' said Lord Henry, 'and he was still at Merton with Lady H. when I left England. But Admiralty will employ him when the time comes, depend upon it.'

Dacres frowned and blew a thin drift of smoke.

'I dare say the mob have faith in Nelson,' he said, 'but I can't say I have. One of your impulsive sort. Jervis, or Howe, would be my preference for a fleet commander.'

'Jervis is retired and Howe is dead,' observed Lord Henry mildly.

'I'm aware of it,' said the Admiral restively. 'I was merely lamenting our lack of a more solid commander. If there's a big battle, as you surmise, the issue will be damned doubtful, in my opinion. The Spaniards, I know, have been building bigger ships-of-the-line than any we've got.'

'You think the size of a warship gives a marked advantage?'

'It stands to reason, Lord Henry.' The Admiral leaned forward impressively. 'You've never seen two fighting-ships board-and-board. I have. Take one of our biggest, eighty guns, say, and place her alongside a Spaniard of a hundred-and-twenty guns. Now in the first place—'

He continued to expound theories of naval

warfare until it was time for Lord Henry to collect his servant and take his leave.

The carriage clattered down the rough road and through the swarming streets of the port to the quay. The sun was westering, and the eight-mile stretch of the harbour waters glitterd golden under the thickly-wooded slopes that rose above the town. Beyond the forest of masts and spars that stood in dark silhouette against the gold lay the massive bulk of *Theseus*, 74, at moorings, and closer inshore a smaller vessel, three-masted like *Theseus* but much lower in the hull, was anchored. Carberry, as short and plump as his master, jumped out of the carriage to disperse the throng of half-naked piccaninnies that had gathered to stare and Lord Henry descended with more deliberation. As he did so a young man in blue coat and white breeches (a mere boy, he seemed to Lord Henry's eye) stepped forward and doffed his hat.

'Lord Henry Leveson? I'm Hepplewhite, my lord—lieutenant of *Renard*.' He gestured with his hat. 'The cutter waits at the steps yonder, my lord. If your lordship would follow me—Captain Coghlan is anxious to sail before this breeze drops.'

Lord Henry noted with some amusement that Mr Hepplewhite quite evidently considered his captain's anxiety of more importance than the convenience of the Governor of Barbados.

'My baggage, Mr Hepplewhite?' he queried.

The lieutenant cast a quick glance at the trunk and boxes Carberry was unloading from the carriage and turned to shout across the quay.

'Coxswain! Four men here, lively!—Your lordship's man will direct them, my lord,' he added to Lord Henry as four burly seamen came trotting up. 'Perhaps your lordship will come with me.'

He led the way, manifestly restraining impatience, to the steps at the quay's edge. Lord Henry never hurried, and they arrived simultaneously with Carberry and the baggage-carriers. Trunk and boxes were stowed and Carberry ensconced in the bows of the cutter.

'If your lordship will allow me,' said Mr Hepplewhite, stepping down into the sternsheets and offering a hand.

'Thank you,' said Lord Henry. 'And Mr Hepplewhite,' he added in an undertone as he took his seat, 'it would be sufficient, I think if you were to call me "sir".'

'Very good, my—sir.' The lieutenant relieved his embarrassment in a peremptory shout. 'Bow! Shove off. Oars. Give way.'

The cutter slid away from the quay and headed towards the small three-master. The shore scents of Kingston—spice and molasses mingled with less savoury odours—gave place to the salty freshness of the evening breeze. Lord Henry's critical glance examined boat and boat's crew. When he had come ashore from *Theseus* it had been in the captain's gig, the boat glistening with new red and white paint and her crew dressed in gay shirts of red-and-white chequer. *Renard*'s eight-oared cutter, black-painted, had no gaiety about her and the oarsmen wore much-mended canvas trousers and jerseys of varying hues; but the thwarts, he noted, were scrubbed to spotless whiteness and the men clean and cheerful. Peering ahead past the row of faces, bearded or clean-shaven brown, he could see the nearing flank of *Renard* with its eight gunports spaced along the horizontal white streak on her black hull.

'Oh Gemini!' said Lieutenant Hepplewhite beside him, under his breath but quite audibly. 'My—sir, I forgot to present Captain Coghlan's compliments and he looks forward to welcoming you aboard. I—I trust you'll overlook my negligence, sir?'

His concern was so apparent that Lord Henry could not forbear a little mischief.

'And if I do,' he retorted, assuming an air of severity, 'you escape a reprimand, perhaps a charge of disobeying orders, from this captain of yours. Is that it?'

'N-no, sir, indeed!' stammered Mr Hepplewhite, aghast; then he perceived the twinkle in Lord Henry's eye and blushed. 'But it's true enough,' he added stoutly, 'that any kind of negligence displeases Captain Coghlan.'

'Ha. A hard man, I see. One of your flogging captains, doubtless.'

'Nothing of the sort!' Hepplewhite forgot the 'sir' in his indignation. 'Beg pardon, your lordship, but if you've heard that anywhere it's a lie. Ask any officer or seaman in *Renard*.'

'Oh,' said Lord Henry blandly. 'You would say, then, that he is a good captain?'

'The best!' cried the young man enthusiastically. 'There's not another in the service to match him for—'

He checked himself in a hurry, suddenly aware that he was guilty of confiding in a stranger, and covered his confusion by standing up at the tiller to bring the cutter alongside.

There was no entry-port and gangway at the sloop's side, but it was only a climb of a dozen feet up the rope-ladder to the break in the midships rail and Lord Henry made the ascent without mishap. A double rank of marines, six a side, presented muskets as he set foot on *Renard*'s deck. A tall man with a single gold-braided epaulette on the left shoulder of his blue coat stepped forward hat in hand; a lean unsmiling hawk-face, Lord Henry noted, and black hair thickly streaked with grey.

'Welcome aboard, sir,' said Jeremiah Coghlan.

2

His majesty's sloop *Renard*, of eighteen guns, was a ship-rigged three-master carrying main courses, topsails, topgallants and royals like any seventy-four. Three jibs and a driver completed her sail-plan and gave her something of the look of a scaled-down line-of-battle ship, but the length of her hull, which was quarter-decked aft, was under 120 feet not counting the forty-foot bowsprit. On her main deck were the sixteen 18-pounder carronades, eight to a side, and two long 6-pounders were mounted as bow and stern chasers. In the eighteen months he had commanded her she had made her way into Jeremiah Coghlan's affections.

Jeremiah had come very near to settling into a soured and disappointed middle-age. Once the pangs of his loss had become dulled and the memory of Trenythan no more than a fantastic dream he had devoted himself to his profession as a sea-officer, at first in half-realised but savage desire to revenge himself on the Fate that had at a blow deprived him of Margaret and of the prospect of social advancement; if he could not rise by that staircase there still remained the quarterdeck ladder, once more beneath his feet by the turn of events. To be made post was all his ambition now, and he swore to himself that he would win the coveted step by his own merits and energies alone, with no patronage even from Admiral Sir Edward Pellew.

Pellew, at sea since the resurgence of the war, was in any case on the other side of the world, commanding in the East Indies. He would probably have been able to arrange the fulfilment of Jeremiah's consuming desire, which was appointment to a frigate serving in the Channel or the Mediterranean where fighting and promotion were most likely to be found.

As it was, Jeremiah had no choice but to accept his appointment as third lieutenant of *Vanguard*, 74, sailing to join Sir John Duckworth's squadron in the West Indies. That he was lucky to get such an appointment he knew very well; but that did not prevent him from feeling frustrated and ill content as *Vanguard* bore him farther and farther from what Lord Henry Leveson had rightly called 'the arena of decision'.

His promotion to second lieutenant, Captain Bligh's original second having died of fever, did nothing to rid him of the sullen humour that was fast becoming his customary mood. When, after the action with *Seduisant*, Admiral Duckworth had promoted him master and commander into the ship-sloop *Renard* he had seen in this only the final blow to his ambitions; *Renard* would never leave the Caribbean, nor was she ever likely to fight an action that could lead to her commander being made a post-captain.

It was partly his own natural resilience, partly increasing pleasure in his new command, that brought Jeremiah slowly out of his crabbed discouragement. Post-captain he might not be, but captain he was, able to make what he could of a fast and handy ship. He had but one lieutenant and he a callow youngster, but under him were Chivers the white-bearded master, a purser and a surgeon, Lieutenant Brewster and Sergeant Pratt and their dozen red-coated marines, a boat-swain, a carpenter, and a gunner. *Renard*'s lower-deck was below her proper complement—seventy men instead of ninety—but they had served together as a crew for more than a year and there were no landsmen or gaolbirds to be hammered into seamen. Shutting his mind firmly against the past and its might-have-beens, he began to devote himself to moulding *Renard* into a completely efficient fighting-ship.

Edward Pellew had kept his place in Jeremiah's thoughts as the ideal sea-officer, and now he recalled Pellew's example and precepts and tried to follow them. Admiral Dacres, newly appointed to the West Indies command, made no secret of his personal dislike for the sloop's commander on the few occasions when they met, and the dislike was reciprocated. Jeremiah knew he could expect no commendation from his admiral. But at least Dacres did not interfere with the internal running of the ships in his command, and *Renard*'s orders—to harass the enemy's merchant shipping and attack enemy privateers—gave her a great deal of independence.

These orders related mostly to cruising in the eastern Caribbean, where the 500-mile long chain of the Leeward and Windward Islands alternated French possessions with British and privateers preyed constantly upon the British trade; and since a thousand miles of sea, sometimes storm-swept and some-times placidly blue, lay between Jamaica and *Renard*'s cruising-ground she was not often in Kingston harbour. Before Jeremiah had completed his first cruise in her his ship's company knew that they had a captain who brooked no indiscipline, flogged sparingly but without mercy for thieves or laggards—and had a bee in his bonnet concerning gunnery.

One saying of Pellew's Jeremiah had taken particularly to heart: *Train your gun-crews until they can load and run-out in their sleep*. His gun-drill was so persistent that in a month he had almost achieved this. In Mr Timms the gunner, a small thin man wearing steel-rimmed spectacles, he had an ardent assistant.

'Acc'racy,' declared Mr Timms (it was his watchword), 'acc'racy's the thing. Every ball where it's intended to go. Do the job by gunnery—that's what it's for, to do away with this silly business of boarding.'

Firing at a target was his specific for accuracy, and his captain, fully approving, was constantly pestering the naval armament stores of the eastern Caribbean ports for powder and shot. Fourteen French and Spanish merchantmen had been taken by *Renard* and brought into port before this stringent exercising received a proper test. The brief duel between the ship-sloop and the more heavily-armed privateer *Candide* ended in the Frenchman's capitulation with main and foremasts gone, poop shot to pieces, and half her company dead or wounded. *Renard* had one man killed and another wounded, and a hole or two in her canvas.

This successful action completed what Jeremiah Coghlan's forceful personality had begun. *Renard*'s crew saw themselves and their ship and their captain as a single entity designed to triumph over all assaults of sea, storm, and Frenchmen. There had been no floggings since that date. Young Mr Hepplewhite, still of an age for hero-worship, developed a dual personality. The puppyish naiveté natural to his nineteen years was replaced on the quarterdeck by the stern bearing and keen eye for faults of a first lieutenant, and if his harsh voice and grim-set jaw were rather too patently modelled on those of his senior he had in fact made himself (under Jeremiah's careful tuition) a very capable officer.

As for Jeremiah Coghlan himself, he was sufficiently happy. He liked his men and loved his ship; and though the consciousness of missing opportunity was always there he could forget it in the crowding responsibilities of command. He remained taciturn and somewhat aloof, graver of bearing than his thirty years seemed to warrant. But his mouth had lost its sour twist and his mind the shadow that had settled upon it in the stable-yard of Trenythan Hall three years ago.

Jeremiah's taciturnity concealed a certain impatience, however. The encounter with *Candide* had been the only sea-fight worth the name in eighteen months, and he felt that in firing shots across the bows of French merchantmen the highly efficient fighting machine he had brought into being was wasted. He wanted another action with a warship of equal force, or against odds, to test himself and his ship. That Captain Coghlan nursed hopes of such an action was revealed to his distinguished passenger on the fourth day out from Kingston.

Lord Henry had found the first forty-eight hours of the voyage somewhat trying. A few leagues east of Gallows Point *Renard* had run into bad weather, a minor storm with intermittent rain-squalls that persisted for two days. He considered himself a fair sailor, and in *Theseus* had suffered no inconvenience once Madeira was astern; but the more violent motion of the smaller vessel troubled him sorely and he kept his cabin. It was in fact the captain's cabin. Quarters on board *Renard* were tight, and though the captain's cabin below the quarterdeck was the largest in the ship it was by no means a grand affair.

'Mr Hepplewhite and I keep watch-and-watch at sea,' Jeremiah had explained when Lord Henry had demurred—not too forcibly—at such sacrifice. 'One cot between the two of us is enough.'

Carberry's expert ministrations assisted his master in a rapid recovery, and on the third evening of the voyage Lord Henry was able to accept the captain's invitation to dine with him in the tiny stateroom and even to deal enjoyably with a morsel of excellent steak. The fare, he noted, was plain but not as Spartan as the admiral had led him to expect; and there was a very drinkable Spanish wine, taken from one of *Renard*'s prizes, to oil the wheels of conversation.

Captain Coghlan should be called laconic rather than unsociable, Lord Henry decided. He replied to questions and volunteered statements but never with any amplification. He was ready enough to talk about his ship and the present voyage when his passenger asked about them, remarking with satisfaction that after the recent blow the wind had veered southerly, so that he could for the time being hold a straight course east by south for Barbados. He could even laugh, as he did when Lord Henry, feeling happier after his third glass than he had felt for three days, repeated Canning's latest quatrain, on the Government's anti-invasion blockhouses at the mouth of the Thames:

'If blocks can a nation deliver
   Two places are safe from the French:
The one is the mouth of the river,
   The other the Treasury Bench.'

But only once that evening did the prospective Governor get a glimpse of a deeper sensibility behind the outward polite laconism of Captain Coghlan. Lord Henry, more talkative than his host, had been commenting upon the tiny defence vessels contemptuously described as 'a mosquito fleet' by Sir Edward Pellew in Parliament.

'And Ned Pellew should know what he's talking about,' he said. 'You've served under him, Captain, I understand.'

For the first time he saw the captain's dark eyes light with enthusiasm.

'I have, sir,' Jeremiah said quietly. 'Everything I am and have I owe to Sir Edward.'

But that was all. The meal ended with both men well pleased with each other and an agreement to dine together on the following evening.

Weather more appropriate to a Caribbean summer had followed on the heels of the storms, and Lord Henry pottered about on deck for most of that day. More sociable—and perhaps more truly democratic—than Captain Coghlan, he talked with any man who had leisure for conversation and inquired into any shipboard activity he was not acquainted with. *Renard*, with all her canvas spread, had a strong and steady breeze between bow and beam and was heading as close to the wind as she could lie. The crinkled blue of the sea stretched far away under a cloudless sky, and at intervals a silver fountain of spray glittered transiently above the for'ard rail before falling with a wet clatter on the deck.

A continuous metallic chinking drew Lord Henry for'ard, where he found Mr Timms, the gunner, directing half-a-dozen seamen who were squatting by the weather rail hammering away at round-shot. Each ball was passed to the gunner for inspection before it was tossed into a netting slung below the rail.

'Eighteen-pounder shot, m'lord,' said Mr Timms in answer to Lord Henry's question. 'Chippin' all the rust and corrosing orf 'em. Some o' the balls we gets from store you wouldn't believe. Look at this bugg—this 'un.' He displayed a rough-surfaced ball. 'Make an acc'rate shot with that? Not on your life.'

He threw it over into the sea. Lord Henry was impressed.

'You need a perfect sphere for accurate gunnery, I take it,' he said.

'You're dead on target, m'lord.' Timms pushed his spectacles up on his forehead and squinted at his questioner in the bright sunlight. 'Stands to reason. You may get your powder proper, your charge exac', your bore true and your aim puffick, but what's the use if your ball's skew-wiff?'

'Logical enough,' agreed Lord Henry. 'And may I ask, Mr Timms, if you have any expectation of sending these balls against an enemy vessel shortly?'

'Look again, you wall-eyed lubber!' The gunner thrust a round-shot back into the hands of one of his men. 'Knob o' rust as big as your nose!—Beg pardon, m'lord. 'Spectation? Well, I dunno. Hope's the word, I reckon. We all of us hopes to come up with that privateer swab Arbos—specially the captain. Then we'll show him gunnery!'

When dinner was over that evening and they were dealing with some port which Lord Henry had produced from his baggage he mentioned this conversation to Captain Coghlan.

'Admiral Dacres spoke of this Arbos,' he

added. 'His ship is called *General Ernouf*, I gather, a privateer. Is she a—um—powerful vessel?'

'She carries twenty guns and a hundred and sixty men,' said Jeremiah; his eyes were gleaming. 'She's done more damage to our trade in the eastern Caribbean than any half-dozen of the rest.'

'Captain Arbos is efficient, then.'

'He's a good seaman. His tactics are to chase, disable, and board—and *General Ernouf* is the fastest ship in these waters, though she's a ship-sloop like *Renard*.' Jeremiah lifted his glass and frowned at it. 'Twice I've sighted and chased him, but he has the heels of us.'

Lord Henry raised his brows. 'A coward?'

'A wise man,' said Jeremiah. 'His job is to take merchantmen, not to fight warships.'

'And you would give your eyes to catch him, no doubt.'

Jeremiah smiled briefly. 'But not on this voyage, sir. My orders are to deliver your lordship at Bridgetown with all speed and stay for nothing.'

Lord Henry picked up the bottle, examined its remaining contents with a well-accustomed eye, and apportioned them accurately between the two glasses.

'And after my—ah—delivery, will *Renard* return to Kingston?' he inquired.

'No. I'm to cruise northward, off Guadeloupe

and Martinique. *General Ernouf* uses Pointe à Pitre as her base, so we may meet. In fact—' Jeremiah hesitated, with a wary eye on his companion. 'In fact, I have high hopes of our meeting. I've let it be known—Caribbean ports have their own ways of passing-on news—that I shall consider Captain Arbos a poltroon if he doesn't stand and fight next time we meet.'

'A challenge!' cried Lord Henry delightedly. 'Captain Coghlan, I count myself fortunate to have made your acquaintance. You are a living refutation of Pitt's dictum that the age of chivalry is dead. Do you know if any of your ancestors were knights-errant?'

He saw, without understanding it, the sudden tautening of the captain's jaw and the narrowing of the dark eyes.

'I suppose it is possible,' said Jeremiah coldly.

Lord Henry made haste to raise his glass and propose a toast.

'To your meeting with Captain Arbos, sir, and a victorious outcome for *Renard*.' They drank to that, and Lord Henry set down his empty glass. 'A pity,' he added, 'that I shall not be there to see it.'

On the following day *Renard* lost the fair wind that had enabled her to make such good headway and was forced to commence long northerly and southerly tacks. The wind, backing easterly, brought cloudy skies and occasional rain-squalls, and on the rougher days Lord Henry found it more convenient to dine (or not, as his stomach decreed) in his cabin. Whenever less disturbing weather allowed he dined with the captain; his respect and liking for Jeremiah Coghlan increased with each day of the voyage.

By the end of the first week at sea he was a familiar and popular figure both aft and for'ard. Any shipboard activity, whether it was making or shortening sail or the daily gun-drill, was sure to have his tubby but not unimpressive form in attendance, careful to keep out of the way but keenly observant. And everything he observed excited his admiration.

Lord Henry, though no seaman, was by no means ignorant of warships and their ways. He had made voyages in other vessels besides *Theseus*. And he had never come across such unanimity as he found in *Renard*. All her company—the hands, the petty officers, even the stolid marines—seemed as much a part of the ship as her spars and cordage. It was not difficult to perceive that the factor that bound them thus together was their respect and affection for their captain. Spotless decks, gleaming cannon, the eagerness to obey an order promptly and efficiently, all stemmed (in Lord Henry's opinion) from the circumstance that Jeremiah Coghlan was one of those in whom authority is inherent, a born leader of men. Edward Pellow was one of the two or three other such men he had known, and political animosity had sent Ned on a goose-chase to the East Indies instead of to the European waters where England's best sea-officers would soon be in demand. It seemed to Lord Henry that Captain Coghlan, too, was being wasted in this petty warfare so far from what he had called the arena of decision.

The morning of the eleventh day dawned wet and windy, but by noon the sun was clear of clouds and the wind, from east-south-east, had moderated to a steady breeze. Mr Chivers the master put *Renard*'s position at about 200 miles west of St Lucia by dead-reckoning. Lord Henry lunched somewhat more amply than usual, the weather of yesterday having prevented him from dining, and at six bells of the afternoon watch was on deck watching the operation of putting-about as the sloop turned from the southerly leg of her zigzag course and headed north-easterly.

Thereafter he mounted to the quarterdeck (he had the captain's standing invitation to do so when he wished) and scanned the empty circle of the sea. They had spoken only one vessel, a brig Jamaica-bound from St Vincent, since leaving Kingston, for the inter-island trade-routes were far to north or south of their course.

The sky was hazy blue and the horizon less distinct than it had been a few days ago. Lord Henry, standing beside Captain Coghlan at the taffrail, had just remarked that the wind seemed to have dropped a little when the high shrill call came from the masthead.

'Deck, there! Sail, fine on th' labb'd bow!'

The captain's harsh shout answered. 'What d'ye make of her?'

A pause, then: 'Can't see but her tops'ls, sir. Three-master.'

With a terse 'By your leave, sir' Jeremiah caught his glass from the shelf under the taffrail, limped down from the quarterdeck, and ran up the mainshrouds.

'I wish I could climb like that,' said Lord Henry, gazing aloft with his head tilted back.

'Yes, sir,' agreed Lieutenant Hepplewhite, also at gaze. 'Climbs like a damned monk—' He converted the second syllable into a cough. 'Believe me, sir,' he added more decorously, 'what a man—any man—aboard this ship can do Captain Coghlan can do better.'

'I believe you,' returned Lord Henry gravely. 'Except, perhaps, to amputate a leg as expertly as the surgeon.'

Hepplewhite grinned. 'I wouldn't put even that past him, sir. Floyd's a good fellow, but you don't get topnotchers in the surgery line in a ship-sloop. I'm willing to bet—'

He stopped as Jeremiah crossed the deck and

came up the quarterdeck ladder.

'Friend or enemy, captain?' inquired Lord Henry, his quick eye noting the slight frown on the captain's face.

Jeremiah paused before replying, and then spoke formally.

'The vessel yonder is the French privateer *General Ernouf*, Lord Henry,' he said evenly. 'She is heading—'

'Good God, man!' cried Lord Henry excitedly. 'Are you sure?'

'Quite sure, sir. She is heading to intercept our present course. My orders are to avoid action with enemy ships. I therefore intend—'

'Avoid action! But you can't man!' Lord Henry's little eyes were gleaming. 'She can outsail *Renard*, as you yourself told me.'

'If I go about and run for it with a following wind,' Jeremiah continued in the same level tone, 'she may not overhaul us until darkness has fallen. We would then have good hope of evading her.'

'But—' Lord Henry walked a pace away and a pace back. 'Captain Coghlan,' he said severely, 'it is perfectly clear to me that *Renard* has no chance at all of escape. Your only course—your only course, sir—is to fight. And so—mark my words, sir—I would testify at any subsequent court-martial.'

Jeremiah stared for a moment, saw the twinkle in Lord Henry's eye, and smiled.

'It gives me great pleasure,' he said solemnly, 'to find myself of the same opinion as your lordship.'

3

Renard had altered course, heading almost due north with the wind just abaft her starboard beam. Her bowsprit was pointing rather to the left of the French ship now, and Lord Henry could see no reason for this. In the twenty minutes that had passed since the privateer was sighted she had come hull-up from the deck, and his little perspective glass showed her plainly; she was, he thought, a larger and taller vessel than *Renard*, a fine sight under full sail with her dark-red hull and the white band chequered with red gun-ports. There was something going on aloft—she was taking-in her royals.

'She's puzzled,' muttered Lieutenant Hepplewhite at his elbow. 'Wonders why we're heading to cross astern of her.'

'I confess I'm in the same case,' returned Lord Henry.

They both spoke in lowered tones instinctively, though there was noise enough from wind and sea to drown their voices and the captain was out of earshot. Jeremiah was standing immobile at the corner of the taffrail with his glass to his eye. He had not taken his attention from *General Ernouf* once in the past five minutes.

The ship-sloop had been cleared for action, but (to Lord Henry's surprise) there had been no beating to quarters, no rumble of gun-tracks as the 18-pounders were loaded and run out. The dozen marines, indeed, had come trotting up to their action stations on the poop, and their bright red jackets and white crossbelts were neatly aligned along the rail on either side; Lieutenant Brewster, a stocky man with ginger whiskers, stood against the after-rail tapping the deck impatiently with the tip of his scabbard. The gun-crews were grouped at their weapons, the shot was ready in the nettings and the matches smouldering in their tubs, but the gunports remained closed.

'She's going about,' said Hepplewhite suddenly.

There could be no doubt of the privateer's intention to fight. Perceiving that *Renard* would cross her wake on the present course, she came round before the wind to make sure of intercepting her. Now she was less than two miles ahead and the British ship, with a beam wind, was closing the distance rapidly.

'Almost long gunshot,' said Hepplewhite, trying to conceal his excitement in a nonchalant drawl. 'You see the strategy, sir? The captain wants the weather-gauge. So first we convince

Monsieur that we're about to attack—'

'Mr Hepplewhite,' the captain's harsh voice interrupted, 'I'll have her stripped to tops'ls, if you please.'

'Aye aye, sir!'

Hepplewhite sprang forard, bawling orders. The gun-crews were instantly in swift controlled movement, a stream of men swarming aloft. *Renard*'s royals, topgallants, and main courses disappeared from her yards as if by magic. She wore only her fighting canvas now. Jeremiah had lowered his glass but had not taken his gaze from the Frenchman, who was so close that movement on her deck could be discerned. Her upper and main sails were being taken-in as she prepared for the imminent engagement. Lord Henry gulped. At any moment Captain Arbos might try a long shot, and up here on the quarterdeck he felt extremely conspicuous. The captain's trenchant shout made him jump.

'Make all sail! Sheets and braces, there! Mr Chivers, hard over!—Keep her so!'

With incredible swiftness *Renard*'s three masts blossomed with their full burden of sails again, and simultaneously she spun on her heel, to go racing away on the larboard tack close-hauled. The privateer, taken by surprise, hastily went about and re-hoisted her lowered canvas, but by the time she had way on her *Renard* had made good sufficient distance to place her nearly due south of her adversary, and in another few minutes was turning to larboard with the wind over her quarter, her bows pointing straight at *General Ernouf*. She had won the weather-gauge.

'Mr Hepplewhite,' said Jeremiah, 'strip to topsails, if you please.'

Once again, and with a rapid precision that made Lord Henry open his eyes, the ship-sloop's canvas was reduced to topsails only. At a word from the captain one of Brewster's marines took a stiff pace forward and produced a deafening *rafale* from the small drum slung from his neck, sending every man to his battle-station.

'All guns—load and run out!'

And now at last came the thunderous vibration of the trucks, the quick sharp voices of the gun-captains reporting their weapons ready. And then a silence in which could be heard the faint song of the wind in *Renard*'s rigging and the ripple of water along her side as she moved steadily, but more slowly under her reduced sail, towards her enemy. The privateer, also under topsails, was no more than a mile ahead and broadside-on, her motion through the water almost imperceptible. Lord Henry, who could see the black squares of her open gunports quite plainly, felt a strong impulse to dash below decks.

'We shall engage very shortly, sir. You would

be well advised to leave the deck.' The captain had turned to speak to him. 'It's likely to be a hot action.'

Lord Henry surveyed the calm hawk-face (it wore a little smile, he noticed) and swallowed his apprehensions.

'I'd prefer to stay where I am, captain,' he said.

Jeremiah's smile became a grin. 'As you will, sir,' he said. 'I should warn you that we'll have to stand fire.'

'How so?'

'Arbos would have run down from windward and tried to board—his usual tactics. I've spoiled that by getting the weather-gauge. Now he'll try for my spars as soon as he's within range.'

'But you'll reply?'

'No. My gun-captains are trained to aim precisely, Lord Henry. I shall fire only when every gun can be certain of hitting its target.—Pray excuse me.' Jeremiah went to the taffrail and leaned over. 'Mr Timms! Larboard broadside. Range will be thirty fathoms, target deck-level and ports. I'll give the word.'

'Aye aye, sir!' squeaked Timms from the main-deck.

Lord Henry looked at the French ship. She was much closer now and he thought he could make out the gun-muzzles in those yawning ports. Discovering that he was trembling, he steadied himself with both hands on the rail. A moment later he saw a bright flash below the Frenchman's rail and something screeched through the air just above his head, making him duck. Before he had recovered there was a second flash and bang, quickly followed by a rapid series of discharges.

A splintering crash made him turn, and he saw *Renard*'s cutter, slung amidships with the ship's longboat, knocked into a flurry of splinters. In the mizzen topsail above him two round holes had appeared. He looked for Hepplewhite and espied him sauntering along behind the maindeck guns with his hands clasped behind his back. Steadily *Renard* crept towards the Frenchman, while the irregular gunfire roared louder and louder from the red-and-white hull.

'Very well, Mr Brewster,' said Jeremiah.

'Load!' snapped Brewster, and the long ramrods of the marines glinted in the sunlight.

Another crash, and another. A ball scored a white groove on the lower mainmast and went howling off in ricochet. The long-boat, a shattered wreck, dangled from its slings. Lord Henry, gripping the rail and very frightened, could actually see the faces of men on board *General Ernouf*. It was too much. It was folly. Why did not Coghlan—

'Hard-a-starboard!'

A bare sixty yards from the privateer, which

was partly hidden now in drifting smoke, *Renard* swung round, presenting her broadside to the red-and-white flank.

'Fire!'

Lord Henry staggered as the deck reeled to a simultaneous discharge. Recovering, he found a cloud of acrid-smelling smoke obscuring his view and glanced down at the main-deck, where the gunners were reloading with extraordinary rapidity. An ear-splitting bang—the marines firing a volley—came before another shattering broadside from the 18-pounders. Something moved above the edge of the smoke-cloud and he saw it was the upper spars of a mast, toppling in a slow arc. Then the smoke blew clear and he saw *General Ernouf*.

The privateer's mizzen-mast was down, banging about in a tangle of cordage. Most of her rail seemed to have gone, two of her gunports were shapeless ragged holes, and dead or wounded men lay in heaps about her deck. *Renard* had drawn past her and the guns of her broadside had ceased to fire, but Lord Henry saw the flash of her fore-chaser and felt the shock as the ball thudded into the stern timbers just below him.

'Ready about!' The harsh voice was calm, impersonal. 'Starboard broadside, Mr Timms—fire as your guns bear. Helm over!'

Renard turned a half-circle and moved slowly back towards her adversary. Lord Henry braced himself for what he knew must come, but even so he was shocked and shaken by the inferno of noise that burst out as the two ships came broadside to broadside again. Half-stunned and wholly deafened though he was, he could grasp the fact that *Renard*'s guns were firing at a far faster rate than the privateer's, and with a deadly accuracy. The uproar ceased as they drew clear again. Looking astern through eddying smoke-wreaths, he gazed past the motionless figure of the captain—erect, hands behind back, intent on the enemy—to see the Frenchman with her decks a shambles, her gunports beaten into jagged gaps, and one of her two remaining masts leaning drunkenly against the other.

'She must strike,' he muttered involuntarily. 'She *must* strike.'

'Ready about!' came Jeremiah's rasping shout. 'Larboard broadside, Mr Timms!'

Renard wore round. Before she had gathered way to re-pass the French ship they saw the tongue of orange flame that wavered up from her after-deck, swiftly leaping higher and widening its base. Instantly Jeremiah snapped an order at the helmsmen and the ship-sloop turned into the wind to lie hove-to a cable's length from her prey. Hardly had she done this when there was a brilliant flash and a tremendous explosion of sound. *General Ernouf* vanished in a great upsurge of black smoke, and above the smoke soared a thousand whirling fragments; fragments of ship and men. When the smoke blew clear they saw, but for a few seconds only, the broken and smouldering hull still above the water. Then she was gone, and the dark-stained waves showed only a litter of broken spars and timbers amid which living men struggled feebly for survival.

Lord Henry was clinging to the rail, stunned by the suddenness of the catastrophe. Voices, crisp and urgent, penetrated his dulled consciousness.

'Only the jolly-boat, sir . . . Sway her out, then, and lively . . . Aft, here, boatswain . . . all small cordage . . . Casks, spars, anything that'll float . . .'

Someone barked an order and the marines went clumping and clanking down to the after-deck. Their going roused Lord Henry from his shocked stupor and restored his mind to its normal inquisitiveness, so that the need to discover what was going on overcame the shakiness of his legs. He lurched across to the taffrail and leaned on it, looking down on the after-deck.

It took him a moment or two to make sense of the busy scene below him. Demoniacal-seeming men, naked to the waist and with blackened faces and chests, were laying out fathoms of stout line and cutting them to varying lengths while others secured casks or pieces of timber to one end. The blackened men, he realised, had been serving *Renard*'s guns only a little while before.

Captain Coghlan was supervising the bringing-alongside of the ship's only remaining boat—the little jolly-boat. Men climbed down into her, the bights of the lines were coiled and tossed down, and the improvised floats thrown overside. Lord Henry discerned the business in hand now and was filled with admiration. With eyes glistening sentimentally he watched the jolly-boat pull laboriously across to the area where *General Ernouf* had sunk.

It was a scene that imprinted itself permanently on his memory. The wind had fallen to the lightest of breezes and the sun was a golden ball in the bank of haze to westward. Over the glitter of slow-heaving water the jolly-boat towed her trailing floats, threading a tortuous course through the flotsam of the vanished privateer. Ever and anon an exhausted man would raise himself in the water and throw an arm over one of the towing spars or fasten his hands round a cask. He saw two men hauled into the jolly-boat, but this was as many as the tiny craft could bear in addition to the oarsmen.

Back she came, and half-drowned men, some of them badly burned, were pulled up onto *Renard*'s deck to be carried below by marines acting as loblolly boys. A second time the boat made her short voyage of mercy, and a third time; but at her third return she carried only one rescued Frenchman inboard and there were none clinging to her floats.

They took fifty-five men from the water after the sinking of *General Ernouf*. The remaining one hundred and five of her crew were lost, including their captain, Arbos.

4

'Upon my soul, it passes belief!' said Lord Henry for the third time. 'You fight a twenty-gun privateer and sink her, and you haven't a single man dead or wounded. By God, it's incredible, captain!'

Jeremiah smiled wryly. 'So the Admiral will say when he reads my report,' he returned.

The two were pacing up and down the little quarterdeck in the fresh breeze that had sprung up just after sunset, Lord Henry's short stride matched by the captain's limp. Astern the western sky showed long swathes of crimson, but the colour that had dyed *Renard*'s sails had faded from them now and they towered pale against the darkening east. Long before sunset the ship-sloop had resumed her voyage, her decks swabbed and orderly, her guns cleaned and secured behind their closed ports. Below decks for'ard Floyd and his assistants were still dealing with the wounds and burns of half-a-hundred rescued Frenchmen, and an intermittent banging somewhere amidships told of work in progress on the four shot-holes and the splintered rail.

'If Dacres doubts your veracity,' exclaimed Lord Henry impetuously, 'I'll confirm every word myself—by God I will!' The bottle of port he had consumed at dinner, feeling he deserved it, increased his ardour. 'I never heard of a more absolute victory. It merits a *Gazette* to itself. It certainly merits a commander's promotion to post rank.'

'Which, however, will not be made,' said Jeremiah.

'And why not, may I ask?'

'*General Ernouf* was not a vessel of the French navy. She was a warship chartered to fight in the French cause, a privateer. Admiralty does not recognise an action with a privateer as giving any basis for promotion.'

They had reached the turning-point of their short walk and Lord Henry stopped, taken aback by this information. His companion paced on without pausing and he had to trot after him.

'But that's unbelievable,' he said indignantly when he had fallen into step.

'As unbelievable, perhaps, as my report,' Jeremiah said with a chuckle. 'But it is so.'

'Surely your admiral's recommendation—'

'In my case that's most improbable, sir.'

Lord Henry had nothing to say to this, but his sense of justice was injured.

'It's ridiculous!' he burst out. 'A victorious action such as this should be made public—the nation should know of it, sir. In particular the succouring of your foes when the conflict was over. There you followed precisely the Christian precept, captain.'

'A precept preached by an old friend of yours, sir,' said Jeremiah. '"As long as he can fight back a Frenchman's an enemy to be killed. When his ship's gone he's a life to be saved." Captain Pellew said that in my hearing and I've never forgotten it.'

'Ah,' said Lord Henry. 'Indeed. Um.'

He paced in silence for two turns of the quarterdeck, reflecting. Intervention with Dacres? Against protocol and unprofitable. Direct correspondence with Admiralty by the Governor of Barbados? The same applied; Lord Henry could imagine their Lordships' reaction when a civilian, Governor or no, recommended a naval officer for promotion. But there was a surer way here, he was convinced.

'You'll excuse me, captain,' he said, halting. 'It grows chill up here. I'll go below.'

Turning to look back from the head of the quarterdeck ladder he saw Captain Coghlan's tall figure stiff and motionless at the after-rail, in black silhouette against the fading colours of the west.

Down in the cabin Carberry was bidden to light the lamp and bring paper, pen and ink. Lord Henry dipped his quill. He paused for a moment, his round face upturned to the swinging light and settling into firm determination. He began to write.

'*To the Commander-in-Chief of His Majesty's Ships and Vessels in the East Indies.*
'*My dear Ned* . . .'

EPILOGUE

The eleven ships of the Mediterranean Fleet, homeward bound, sighted the Lizard in the early daylight of a clear June morning. By the time the risen sun was sparkling on the lively chop of the Channel waves they had raised Dodman Point on the larboard bow. The great ships sailed in perfect formation, two lines of five with the flagship, the *Caledonia* of 80 guns, in the van. They carried all sail to the royals, a glorious sight with the sun lighting the towers of white canvas and a moderate sou'wester tilting the thirty-three tall masts uniformly to leeward.

On the flagship's quarterdeck the Admiral—Baron Exmouth of Canonteign, Admiral of the Blue—stood with his flag captain gazing across three miles of sea to where another and larger fleet moved slowly on the opposite course; a convoy outward bound for the East Indies, with a single frigate for escort. Today, ten years after Trafalgar, there was no need for powerful escorts, even though Bonaparte, escaped from Elba, was at this moment making a last great bid for victory on land. The two men were watching a white speck of sail fast growing larger against the dark loom of the distant convoy. The frigate *Alcmene* had signalled that she was sending her cutter with dispatches.

'What dispatches can they have for me, a dozen leagues from port?' wondered the Admiral, frowning.

He was a tall man, greyhaired, nearing his sixtieth year. The flag captain, some twenty years younger, was as tall as his senior, though he was lean in contrast with the other's breadth and stoutness.

'She used the code-flag for "dispatches",' he said. 'It could merely mean "news", sir.'

'Aye,' growled Lord Exmouth, still frowning. 'News of Bonaparte, maybe.'

They fell silent, their eyes on the approaching cutter. They knew of the Emperor's swift march northward and of the vast army that had flocked to his banner; in both their minds was doubt as to whether the Allies, dilatory and divided, could meet and avert this lightning stroke.

The cutter came dancing over the waves with the breeze on her beam, executed a neat gybe, and spilled her wind to run level with *Caledonia* twenty fathoms away. A young officer on her deck waved his hat and bawled interrogatively.

'Admiral Lord Exmouth?'

The Admiral, leaning over the rail, raised his arm.

'Captain Brett's compliments, my lord,' yelled the lieutenant, 'and I'm to give you the news—a great victory—Wellington's licked Boney—place called Waterloo!'

The cutter was drawing ahead despite her crew's efforts. The Admiral took off his own hat and waved it aloft.

'Huzza for Wellington!' he shouted. 'My thanks to Captain Brett—and *bon voyage!*'

As the cutter swung away close-hauled he turned to the flag captain and held out his hand. His face, deep-lined and ruddy, was smiling and his brown eyes agleam.

'You know what this means, Jerry my lad?' he said. 'Peace—and a lasting peace this time.'

Jeremiah Coghlan's smile was less enthusiastic but his grasp of the proffered hand was hard and firm.

'And by the Lord!' Edward Pellew went on hastily. 'We'll be off Rame Head in a brace of shakes—I must see my secretary.' He turned and paused a moment. 'But my invitation stands. You'll dine with me and Lady Exmouth at West Cliff House tonight.'

'I shall be honoured, sir,' said Captain Coghlan.

When the Admiral had left the quarterdeck his eyes sought the cutter, now half-a-mile away and speeding back to the convoy. Nineteen years ago it had been, that other cutter making back to a convoy when he had been a youngster in the brig *Colombe*. That had been not so far from *Caledonia*'s present position—and come to think of it, other links with the past were not so far away, either. Bridport (and he must look up old Abner at the first opportunity) was fourteen leagues and more away, beyond the Start, but Polruan lay only a dozen miles nor'-nor'-east. From the masthead, no doubt, his glass would be able to pick out Trevarder farm on its hilltop; Tom Cargis was dead now, and his daughter Susan lived there with a husband and nine children. And beyond was Trenythan Hall.

He thought of Margaret, and without pain. She was Mrs Trenear these nine years. And Charles Paddon, he had heard, had left the Navy and was something or other with the Embassy in Brussels. He had no wish to meet either of them again and did not expect to.

Six clangs from the flagship's bell told him that it was seven o'clock and brought him back to the present. He glanced round *Caledonia*'s roomy quarterdeck—his own quarterdeck. The three midshipmen, *point-device* as to uniforms and hats, very conscious of his eye; the two lieutenants (he had five under him) pacing the lee side and careful not to intrude on his own pre-empted territory of the deck; the enormous flag rippling out from its jackstaff. The breeze swung the loop of gold braid and stirred the tassels of his epaulettes. Jeremiah Coghlan, ship's boy and bastard, had not done so badly for himself.

He laid a hand on the polished teak of the rail

and felt the transmitted vibration of sea and wind like the pulse of a living thing. His love lay beneath his palm. Ships were his mistresses, and always would be. For the end of the war would not mean the end of employment for Admiral Lord Exmouth's flag captain, though it meant the end of his hard climb; on the list of post-captains there were six hundred and ninety-three names ahead of his, and though he lived through another half-century of peace he would never reach admiral's rank.

A brief but delicious smell of coffee came to his nostrils and reminded him that he had not yet breakfasted. He cast a keen glance astern.

'Mr Fraser!' he barked. 'Make "Flag to *Valiant*: keep better station."'

'Aye aye, sir,' said Fraser smartly, and turned to snap orders at the signal midshipman.

No, reflected Captain Coghlan, he had not done so badly for himself. He limped down the quarterdeck ladder to his cabin.